Agents of Winter

Ada Maria Soto

ROOKERY

Rookery Publishing

Rookery Publishing

Agents of Winter

ISBN: 978-1-99-117860-2 (EPUB)

ISBN: 978-1-99-117861-9 (PDF)

ISBN: 978-1-99-117862-6 (Kindle)

ISBN: 978-1-99-117863-3 (Amazon Print-on-Demand Paperback)

ISBN: 978-1-99-117865-7 (Paperback, New Zealand)

ISBN: 978-1-99-117864-0 (Print-on-Demand via Draft2Digital)

ISBN: 978-1-99-117866-4 (Dyslexia Friendly Edition, Amazon Print-on-Demand Paperback)

Contents

Author's Note

Somewhere around 2011 I had a flash of an image. A man in a suit sitting on the edge of a hospital bed. Over the next six years that image slowly spun itself out into the story of Martin and Arthur and became *His Quiet Agent*. I submitted it to my publisher at the time only to have it rejected. It was then rejected by a few other agents and publishers for 'not being a romance', or 'we wouldn't know how to market this'.

In 2017 I decided to self-publish fully expecting absolutely no one to read it. I literally did it as an exercise to teach myself the steps of self-publishing. Instead, people read it. Not all at once but ever so slowly, through word of mouth, *His Quiet Agent* snowballed.

In the last five years I've gotten a lot of feedback. Most of it positive, a little negative, and many people wanting more. People have especially wanted more of Martin's story. Well, here you have it. I know it took me five years (and a prescription of Ritalin) to get it done, but the first took me six years so if anything, it's ahead of schedule.

This story does go into past death of a parent, a child living in unstable environments with substance abuse taking place, uncomfortable holiday meals with family, and has on page migraines and panic attacks.

It's also a slice of life story mostly about the boys having a nice little vacation together over the winter holidays. So, there's a little angst in the fluff but it's mostly fluff.

Also, the library kids are back and better than ever.

For all of us who forget that handshakes are a thing until there is an empty hand in front of us and an awkward silence.

Chapter One

THE AGENCY HAD COMMITTED many sins in its years of operation. Those sins were kept behind lock and key and encryption; stamped with words like Top Secret and Eyes Only. These sins and crimes were hidden even from the agents who helped create them.

There was only one sin in the organization that every agent had access to, and full knowledge of, no matter their rank or position: Sub-level three, the cafeteria. Placed above the servers (supposedly) and below the room of high-tech gadgets (rumored), it was a location that Arthur seldom visited and not just because he preferred his own cooking. On the rare occasion when an unexpected late shift forced him to pop down for a coffee and a plastic- wrapped white bread sandwich, the quality had reminded him of school lunches. Possibly a little worse.

He wasn't sure if Martin had ever been to the cafeteria, as he subsisted on apple slices prior to their meeting and now mostly ate what Arthur fed him. However, one day a year, perhaps out of patriotism, or maybe shame, the cafeteria put on an excellent Thanksgiving spread for those who either had to work or who volunteered so others could be at home with family.

He slid down the line with two plates, one for himself and one for Martin. There had been a slight widening of Martin's eyes that Arthur recognized as confusion and possibly overwhelming panic as he was confronted with the Thanksgiving buffet.

He didn't ask if Martin had ever had a Thanksgiving dinner before, knowing the answer would either be no, a long time ago, or not in this form. Instead, he'd taken two plates and sent Martin off to sit with Carol.

Martin's plate looked more like a small Thanksgiving-themed charcuterie board with bits of this and that minus certain flavors and textures he knew Martin wouldn't like. For himself, he piled up the starch, added a couple pieces of turkey, and drowned the whole thing in gravy. There were times for bringing out the restaurant presentation skills, then there was his own Thanksgiving plate.

He slid Martin's plate in front of him. Carol didn't comment, but Carol was good that way. In the months that Martin was missing on that disastrous assignment, she'd been the closest thing he had to a shoulder to cry on, giving her a better understanding of his relationship with Martin than anyone else.

She did, however, look over Arthur's plate of starch covered in meat juice. "If I ask about a vegetable, will I sound like your mother?"

"It's Thanksgiving, the only acceptable vegetables are green beans that have been cooked in Campbell's cream of mushroom soup, covered in fried onions, and baked until they lose all nutritional value."

"And here I thought you were Mister Fancy Pants 'I was working in a restaurant when I was five.'"

"I am and I was, but there are exceptions, and this is one of them." He glanced over at Martin, who was studying his plate, his fork hovering over the cranberry sauce with some suspicion. That was the only thing Arthur was unsure of as Martin didn't seem to enjoy foods that might fall under the category of sticky. He hadn't even bothered to put mashed potatoes on the plate. "Spread a bit of it on the turkey. It balances the flavors."

He wouldn't have said anything in front of anyone but Carol. While the rest of the Agency had warmed up to Martin a little, (mostly based on rumors that his injuries had come from doing some

James Bond-level shit that the other analysts could only dream of), Martin valued his privacy and was still uncomfortable with too much interaction.

Martin delicately spread a bit of the cranberry sauce on a small bit of turkey and took a bite. He chewed slowly, as he did with all new foods, before giving a small nod and taking another bite.

"How's Argentina going?" he asked Carol after watching Martin take a few more bites.

Carol shrugged. "Slowly. Chasing up rumors of farmers who found funny bone- shaped rocks a century ago. Living off of barbeque and maté."

"The exciting life of a paleontologist."

Carol lifted her glass in a mock toast.

"When she returns, I am sure the children would enjoy an update as to any discoveries," Martin commented.

"I'll pass that along. She enjoys an audience that isn't her direct competition for grant money. The new research is saying dinosaurs might have honked like giant geese. I'm sure the kids would like to hear about that."

At the Saturday reading hour, the children had loved the lecture on fluffy dinosaurs that Carol's girlfriend gave, even if Arthur ended up with a permanent mental image of a T. rex covered in yellow proto-feathers like some giant Easter chick from hell.

"Geese are evil," Martin stated bluntly, glancing up from his food.

Arthur had no doubt there was a story there, but instead of asking for more, he nodded in agreement and that was the end of the conversation for a while. Technically, they were still on the clock and didn't have that much time to shovel down the turkey. Arthur mostly watched Martin, though, and was proud to see him trying at least a bite of everything and clearing probably half his plate.

Martin's dietitian would be glad as well. Evidently, his comment at his last appointment of 'I currently weigh more than I did prior to the incident' did not paint a good picture of Martin's long-term health management skills. Martin was sent home with an entirely new food plan that Arthur had to rework into meals that Martin could and would eat. It was an ongoing project, but Arthur was patient.

Carol checked her watch. "Well, I've got a load of reports to get back to. Gentlemen, this has been fun and way more pleasant than watching my mother and grandmother get passive aggressive over dressing."

"Dare I ask?" Arthur had strong feelings about dressing.

"Cornbread verses buttermilk biscuit."

"Cornbread."

Carol rolled her eyes. "It's starch, shoved up a turkey. It does not matter."

Arthur turned to Martin. "Cornbread," he repeated.

Martin looked back at him slightly confused but with a hint of a smile.

Arthur knocked on his supervisor's door and waited to be called in. He was sure he hadn't spoken to the man more than twice since the day he was 'promoted' to the fifth floor.

A 'Come in' came faintly through the door and he slid in quickly.

"You wanted to see me, sir?"

"Yes. I have a note from HR that you haven't filled out a B-837 form and they wanted me to nag you about it so consider yourself nagged."

Arthur was confused. He prided himself on filling out necessary paperwork correctly and on time. He filed his taxes in January. "I'm sorry, which one is B-837?"

"Romantic or sexual involvement with another agency employee or contractor."

"I... um..." Arthur felt his cheeks flush and didn't know what to say. It had never crossed his mind to fill out the "Fucking Form" as it was referred to by the crasser employees. His and Martin's relationship had slid from friendship into something deeper and intertwined so smoothly that there was never a date he could point to on a calendar and say 'Yes, here is where our relationship began and I will put that into box 14A.' And, since their calls and messages were monitored, he couldn't argue that he and Martin weren't involved because half the Agency had heard recordings of him leaving sobbing messages on Martin's phone during those months he was missing.

Agent Collins rolled his eyes, certainly misreading Arthur's discomfort. "Look, everyone knows, no one cares. I think there are agents writing romance novels based on you two. Just go fill out the form."

"Yes, sir." Arthur wondered what the Agency's aspiring novelists would say if they knew the two of them mostly cooked, read books, and occasionally went to old movies. "Has Agent Groves filled out a form?"

"How the hell should I know? I'm not his boss."

"Really?" Arthur was of the impression that Agent Collins managed everyone on that wing of the floor.

"He was in that cubicle before I got here and will probably be there when I retire. You probably know more about what he does than I do."

"We don't talk about work."

"Good, you're not supposed to. Go fill out your forms."

Chapter Two

It always started with a pressure in his ears that seemed to amplify the smallest sounds or possibly create ones that weren't even there. Martin blinked at the hard copy text and used one hand like a visor, trying to shield his eyes from the high-rate flicker of the fluorescent bulbs.

The Agency had provided him with top-of-the-line headsets and a screen reader as part of his 'We Fucked Up So Bad You Would Actually Have A Case Even If We Are A Creepy Government Agency So Please Don't Sue Us' compensation. Unfortunately, screen readers were no help when you had to go over page after page of eight-point font photocopied text.

He forced himself to take deep, slow breaths to maximize oxygenation and to unclench his jaw. He had pills he could take but they knocked him out and he had to get this work done. His supervisor wanted a verbal report first thing in the morning, so he just had to get this reading done and he could go home.

He took another deep breath and felt the pressure start to build behind his eyes. He wasn't in pain yet, but he knew it was coming. Every sound seemed unnaturally loud. He could hear the click of Arthur's keyboard only a few feet away. He wasn't typing fast. He'd probably finished his work hours earlier and was simply waiting on Martin now. He could send Arthur a quick message, tell him to go home, say that he still had a lot of work, but it wouldn't have the desired effect. Arthur would stop by his desk, see his face, and know what was happening.

He needed to focus, and then he could get to the pills and maybe knock himself out before the pain left him curled up on the bathroom floor. The doctors assured him that his brain was healing. That he could get through even a few pages of text without a debilitating headache was a positive sign, but that didn't change the fact that he'd never had a migraine in his life until his second week back at the office when he found himself vomiting in pain and unable to open his eyes due to the light.

He finished the last page and slammed the folder into his locking desk drawer with possibly more force than was necessary. He gathered his things quickly, feeling his hands start to shake. Everything seemed to have a sickly green tinge and he felt his stomach begin to turn.

Shit. He hadn't gone fast enough.

"Hey."

He tried to relax his face before he turned to Arthur, but his sudden frown was a clue that he'd failed.

"How bad?" Arthur asked keeping his voice thankfully low.

"I can make it home."

"Okay, let's get you out of here."

Martin fumbled a pair of wraparound dark glasses from his pocket. They let in only enough light so that he wouldn't walk directly into someone, but no more than that. The office was mostly empty with half the lights already turned off, but it was still too much.

Arthur walked at his side, not touching, not adding any stimulation, but close enough to be a comfort or catch him if he fell. They stepped into the elevator, and he felt his stomach lurch as it whisked them down to the garage.

With his glasses on, the garage itself was almost too dark to see. He felt Arthur's hand on his elbow, warm, even through the suit jacket. Arthur guided him to the car so he didn't have to take off the glasses.

The first hints of throbbing pain were beginning to build, a little worse with each pulse.

He let Arthur buckle him in and he squeezed his hands over his ears. He had noise-canceling headphones at home and a blackout eye mask he didn't like wearing.

He bit back a whimper as the closing of the car door shook his whole body. He knew he didn't have to be stoic in front of Arthur. While Arthur hadn't seen him at his worst, he had witnessed the aftermath. Nightmares he couldn't wake from. Physical therapy where his limbs failed to move as they should. Martin tried not to think about it. The car began to move, and he tried to simply focus on breathing through the pain and nausea.

The car moved slowly, Arthur taking each turn wide to minimize the G-forces and crawling to a stop at each light. Martin appreciated what he was trying to do, but it wouldn't be of any use in the end. He counted the turns, trying to mentally distract himself while gauging how much longer he would have to hold it together.

The car came to a halt and the engine stopped, the sudden lack of noise almost as jarring as the rumble of internal combustion. He didn't move. He wasn't sure if he could.

"Should I get your pills and bring them back to the car?"

He feared moving. He feared even breathing. He hated this. Not just the pain but the helplessness. The need for help. For years, he had taken pride in complete self-reliance. Now, if Arthur wasn't there, he would still be reliant on the kindness of strangers. He made no move or sound, fearful of the pain and the reaction of his own body to it.

"Okay," Arthur whispered.

He listened to Arthur get out. The sound of his steps leaving. He took the smallest breaths possible. He knew from experience he couldn't force himself to black out. Even at the most desperate levels of pain, he couldn't hold his breath that long.

The parking lot was quiet, but he could still hear the street noises. As the cars and occasional truck rumbled by, he tried to work out how much time had passed. Had Arthur simply walked away? Decided he had had enough and left him here to figure out his own mess himself? It was a stupid thing to think. Stupid and illogical to even contemplate. Arthur was loyal. It was one of the defining traits the Agency looked for: loyalty and a willingness to serve. For some reason, Arthur had turned that loyalty trait towards him. He wasn't sure why.

He heard footsteps approach the car again. He hoped it was Arthur. He was in no shape to explain his condition to a police officer or innocent bystander, and the only chance he would have of getting away from a kidnapper would be by vomiting on them.

The car chirped as it unlocked, and he winced. His door opened. He couldn't open his eyes to confirm it was Arthur as they were squeezed tight. The muscles of his face seemed locked into place.

"I've got the liquid stuff and your headphones." Arthur's voice was quiet and gentle, yet still hit his ears like a shock wave.

He slowly took his hands from his ears and let Arthur slip on the bulky headphones. They felt like a clamp, but the rough sound of the street became distant and muted. He knew what was coming next. He didn't like it, but there was no other way of relieving this level of pain. He felt Arthur carefully brush aside his suit jacket and untuck his shirt. The air was cold on his bare side, and he gritted his teeth against the quick swipe of cold alcohol on his skin. There was a sharp jab and he bit back a whimper. He knew the puff of warm breath against his skin was a needless apology.

He breathed slowly. This wouldn't fully take away the pain; it was far too late for that. It *should* take the edge off enough for him to get to his apartment and then fall asleep. Hopefully, without a bout of vomiting between those two things.

He felt his muscles begin to relax from the full-body cramp they had constricted themselves into. It must have been some sign to Arthur to start the process of moving him, more delicately than if he was defusing a bomb. Avoiding any sharp movement or noise, he was extracted from his vehicle and helped to his feet. The drugs had taken enough of an effect that he was able to crack his eyes open and make his way.

Arthur took out his keys. He still had the key Martin had given him in the hospital room when he was wracked with fever and afraid of missing his weekly library appointment. He'd never asked for it back and Arthur had never offered. He would have laughed to himself if he wasn't aware of the pain it would cause. So much of their relationship seemed to be centered around him becoming sick or injured. He'd spent years, decades really, striving for near perfect self-sufficiency, then Arthur waltzed into his life and his body decided to completely break down. He supposed the kidnapping and violent aftereffects thereof couldn't be blamed on his body. He knew *exactly* which analyst he could lay the blame on for that and had rather grand plans for eventual revenge.

Arthur led him to his bedroom. "Do you need to use the toilet?"

Martin shook his head. That was a mistake, a big one. He sprinted to the bathroom landing hard on his knees in front of the toilet. His body rejected the sustenance of the day, every muscle screaming in outrage. He became aware of Arthur sitting next to him as he clung onto the cold porcelain. Not touching. He knew not to. Not when every nerve was hyper-aware and tuned to pain.

His body spent another minute trying to reject what wasn't there, simply because it couldn't do anything else. He wanted to cry, but it would serve no purpose in this situation. He had his eyes squeezed tight again, but he could feel Arthur get up, hear the faucet run, and feel a cold glass placed against his fingertips so he knew it was there. He took a sip, more to rinse the taste from his mouth, and felt Arthur sit back down on the hard bathroom floor.

"What are you doing here?" Martin whispered, a heady blend of pain, anger, and self-pity swirling behind his eyes.

"Where else should I be?" Arthur answered back.

With someone who isn't broken, he wanted to reply.

"I filled out a B dash 837 form with HR that has your name on it. I'm exactly where I should be."

Martin reached out and blindly took Arthur's hand because, beneath all the pain, something warm and peaceful bloomed in his chest.

Chapter Three

"So, how are you these days?"

Martin took a deep breath. "I am continually frustrated by the physical aftereffects of my ordeal."

Dr. Francis scribbled a quick note. Appointments with her had ended up a requirement for his return to work. The first few weeks had been difficult. She assumed his lack of communication was due to trauma, not understanding that he'd never been comfortable speaking with strangers. 'Empties' as he'd been taught to think of them as a child, soulless creatures with human forms. Only by putting on a character and a performance could he get through something like the passing of Arthur's father.

After nearly three weeks, he had gritted his teeth and said "I need to know something about you first. Anything."

She had blinked at him and explained that mental health professionals were not supposed to share personal details. Martin hadn't replied to that statement. Maybe some of it was trauma. They kept working.

She had a husband. Played softball in college. Liked cats but was allergic to them. Called them sweet balls of histamine.

"Are you still having migraines?" she asked

"Yes."

She made another note. Actual shorthand she had learned at her mother's insistence. "Have you spoken to your neurologist lately?"

"He said they should eventually fade in severity, but currently they are still easy to trigger."

"Any other triggers?" Dr. Francis asked gently.

Martin sighed internally. He did not like this, at all. "I have an elderly neighbor who is unable to properly clean his apartment. There is sometimes a damp smell that is... particularly unpleasant." It left him gagging, hands shaking with phantom cold, and leg aching in remembered pain. Dr. Francis didn't push for exact details. They had reached an understanding that Martin would acknowledge when he had a problem, and she would in turn acknowledge his acknowledgment.

"Is there anyone who can help him clean?"

"I have offered. He is less social than I am. I have attempted to contact his adult children in hopes that they will handle the matter. If that does not work, I will discuss it with the building manager."

"Hopefully, it won't come to that. Do you have plans for the holidays?"

"I work on Christmas, then spend two or three days in New York attending to legal matters."

Dr. Francis nodded. "Okay, you're in a relationship now. Partners often spend holidays together."

Martin had not considered that. He had filed the appropriate paperwork at the insistence of Human Resources, as had Arthur. He didn't allow himself to stumble over words. He simply did not speak as he considered this new aspect of his life. One of the few sermons he remembered from the Farm was that Silence had Power, especially when dealing with Empties, and that Empties liked to fill the air with words, scared of the power of your silence. As an adult, he understood it was a form of control to discourage gossip among the group and insure as little information as possible was passed from members to outsiders.

It didn't change the fact that one of the things he found interesting about Arthur was his ability to simply sit in silence. Even before that sermon, he had avoided the children who chattered, preferring the quieter ones like himself.

"I shall ask him what his holiday plans are."

Dr. Francis smiled. "Good. That is exactly what you should do."

"May I ask what your holiday plans are?"

Arthur looked up from his soup. The average outdoor temperature had dropped to the point where he had an almost constant rotation of soup on his stove. "Normally, I volunteer to work over the holidays. My mom usually guilts me home every few years. This year I figure I should be a good son and visit my mom, seeing as how she's going to be alone. I have the time saved up. How about you?"

"Historically, I spend the 27th and 28th of December in New York City attending to legal matters. Sometimes the 29th as well."

"Get out before the New Year's Eve madness."

"Yes."

"I've never been to New York. Always been a bit of a bucket list thing. The Met. Ice skating at Rockefeller Center. Broadway. Stupid tourist stuff."

Martin nodded and Arthur wondered exactly what 'legal matters' meant but he didn't push. Martin told him things in his own time, at his own pace. He had a few more sips of soup.

"Would you like to join me in New York? I could extend my visit into the new year with minimal difficulty. I also have considerable leave time saved."

Arthur couldn't stop his smile, not just at the thought of a vacation but at the idea of being somewhere with Martin outside of the spinning routine of the Agency. And an extended stretch of time where he might not feel the need to go through the world wearing the work mask of a cold, unsocial, agent. "You know, I'd like that a lot."

Chapter Four

MARTIN DISMISSED HALF THE library children early to begin their research. The topic was the effect of personal bias on the translation process. He asked several of the older ones to stay and handed each a packet as neatly ordered as any Agency briefing document.

"Over the next few weeks, these are the tasks I wish you to complete, preferably before the winter holiday."

The children opened their packets.

Maria was the first to look up. "School transcripts?"

"Letters of recommendation from our teachers?" Marcel's voice was incredulous.

Lucía shook her head, giving Arthur the impression of a startled cat. "Personal essays?"

"Moving forward, I see no reason why you should continue to suffer through what is called public 'education' in this city, nor be denied what would be offered to children of lesser talent but greater means."

Maria was well into the admissions material for the school Martin had picked for her. "Um... there's no way my mom can afford this place."

"The financial aspect is being taken care of."

"What about my sister?" Julia asked. She had begun bringing her little sister while Martin was away 'slaying dragons.'

"If she continues to progress well, then when it is her time, arrangements will be made."

"There is no way in hell my aunt would let me go to one of these places." Darius held up two brochures. Arthur knew Martin had particularly high hopes and strong plans for him.

"I will speak to any parent or guardian as is necessary."

The children all exchanged looks and several of them cringed. Julia cleared her throat. "Merlin, you know we love you but you're not exactly good at talking with... grownups."

"You clench up really tight and put out a kind of weird vibe," Marcel quickly added. "I mean, it's understandable, most grownups suck, but..."

"I mean there's kinda a reason we all wait outside to get picked up or just walk home," Julia continued while not looking directly at Martin.

Martin sighed, even as Arthur chuckled a little.

"I can fake it when necessary and have been practicing... loosening up."

"He has an outfit that makes him look like Mister Rodgers and lets him charm small town church ladies," Arthur offered by way of reassurance. "My mother thinks he's the 'most delightful young man.'"

"Creepy."

"Surprisingly so."

"Simply do your best to fill out the contents of your packets and inform me next week of any obstacles."

"You really think we could go to these schools?" Julia asked.

"I went to one of those schools and you are all far more advanced than I was at the same age."

"Then how did you get in?"

"My aunt's lawyer wrote a large check and her cook found me a tutor. However, none of you will require tutors."

Marcel shook his head. "You've got a weird life, Merlin."

Martin sighed. "Yes, that has been mentioned."

Chapter Five

ARTHUR BLINKED AND STRUGGLED to reopen his eyes. They felt like they were full of grit. He tried to focus on the newest message on his screen, but the letters were beginning to swim. There was another ping and another line appeared in his inbox with a flag marked urgent. He couldn't be the only analyst who specialized in the region. Yes, things had been a little unstable the last few weeks but they were still months away from a shooting war, by his own analysis. Did all the field agents forget about everyone else? Was there a problem with the filtering system and it was all coming to him? And half of the messages shouldn't have even been red flagged, but there they were.

There were another two pings, each making him jump and each new line was flagged red.

Then a hand gently touched his shoulder. He would have leapt out of his skin in fright if he wasn't so tired.

He turned and looked up at Martin, who looked both rested and put together. "What are you doing here?" Arthur cringed at the slight slur in his voice. "Why haven't you gone home yet?"

"I have gone home. I reheated a serving of the lamb stew for dinner, read a little, slept, and have returned. It is 8:15 in the morning." Arthur turned back to the computer and squinted at the clock. Martin continued, "You have been awake for twenty-six hours."

Arthur wanted to laugh but the sound that came out was more like a short, sharp, sob. There was another ping.

"I just have a few more of these to go through."

Martin gave him a small smile. "I will make you some tea."

Arthur nodded and blinked.

He opened his eyes with his whole body jerking upright. He'd been asleep. He looked around his cubicle. Someone had pushed his keyboard to the side, lowered his chair, and neatly folded a dark gray, almost black, suit jacket into a pillow. There was also a plain white mug of tea. He picked it up with unsteady hands and took a sip. It was oolong and stone cold. He wiggled his mouse.

His computer sprang to life asking for a twenty-character password but also showing the time in the corner.

11:37

Shit!

Arthur typed in his password and got a beep as his shaking hands missed a keystroke.

Okay, breathe. You were not woken by your supervisor yelling at you. You might not get fired.

He started typing again, but in a careful hunt and peck rhythm to ensure accuracy. His inbox had five messages. They were flagged urgent like the rest, but there were only five.

"That can't be right," Arthur muttered to himself. The field reports had been coming fast and thick when he passed out. The last one was marked 8:32. Maybe they started sending the work to other analysts when he stopped responding. He was never sure how those things worked.

He blinked a few more times, then began to read. It wasn't easy, but it was easier. He reached for his cup of cold tea then jerked his hand back. It hadn't burnt him but the cup was warm. He jumped again as he noticed someone standing next to him.

"Hey." His throat felt rough.

"You should drink your tea." Martin's voice was as soft and gentle as he'd ever heard it.

He picked up the fresh cup. It was oolong again. The smell drove some of the cobwebs from his mind. He closed his eyes and took a sip. "Oh, I love you."

He opened his eyes again and Martin was gone.

He tried to run back the last few seconds in his head. Had he said that out loud? Had he ever said that out loud? Did Martin hear him?

He took another sip of tea. He was too tired, and he could feel his autopilot kicking in before he started spinning out into some emotional crisis. Finish work, go home, sleep, wake up, then talk to Martin.

Yep, that was going to have to be the game plan. He drained his cup of tea and got back to work.

It was close to six by the time Arthur hit send on his last report. His typing had slowed to glacial levels as he tried to avoid exhaustion-driven mistakes that could have repercussions down the line.

A gentle hand settled on his shoulder, but he was too tired to even startle properly. It was more of a twitch that ran through his body.

He looked up at Martin. "I will drive us home."

Arthur nodded. He was aware enough to know that he was in absolutely no shape to drive, and trying to get the Agency to reimburse cab fare was a pain in the ass.

"Yeah," was all Arthur said. He quickly logged out and gathered up his stuff while Martin waited. His legs felt wobbly and his head hurt as he followed Martin out of the building. He was asleep, his face pressed against the cool glass of the car window, before they were even out of the parking lot.

It was Martin who put the food in front of him. He had to blink at it a few times, his higher brain functions still running behind everything else. It was a BLT and the smell sent his stomach growling.

"Eat something, then sleep."

That was the plan, eat, sleep, then something? His brain skittered to a halt at anything past eat and sleep.

He picked up the sandwich. A little burnt, a little too much mayo, not quite enough lettuce. It tasted glorious. He managed to mark that Martin was eating a sandwich of his own.

Good.

He felt himself beginning to list forward as he got down to the last bit of crust.

"Time for sleep."

Sleep.

That was the last coherent thought he had before the autopilot fully took over.

This time Arthur woke slowly. He was warm, actually laying down in his own bed, his neck not twisted at an unnatural angle. As his brain slowly turned back on, his awareness grew. His head was only partly on a pillow. Mostly his face was pressed against a hip. He heard a page turn, then felt thin fingers gently comb through his hair. He smiled. Martin almost certainly knew he was awake by the change in his breathing but was willing to let him lay there and drift.

They had the library later, but it couldn't be late enough in the morning yet to justify any rush if Martin was still reading in bed.

A strange tingling thought fluttered around the back of his head. Maybe more memory than thought, but it was proving as ephemeral as a quickly fading dream. He frowned a little and tried to rewind the previous two days in his head. Burnt bacon. Falling asleep in the car. Warm cup of tea cutting through the fog.

Oh.

Arthur opened his eyes and wiggled his way up until he was sitting next to Martin.

Martin finished his page, then looked at him. "Good morning."

Arthur blinked a few times. "I love you." There it was, not grand and romantic but a statement of fact. Something he had known for a while but, like so much of their relationship, never said out loud.

Martin smiled at him. "I know."

"Good. Just wanted to make sure." Martin continued to smile and gave his hand a small squeeze. For Arthur that was enough. He understood the way Martin communicated, at least to an extent. They had said I love you months ago, sitting on a floor, staring at a painting of a cancan dancer. They had just said it in their own way. "Is there any more bacon?" Arthur finally asked, knowing he could waste the day, given half the chance, sitting here next to Martin, but there were children to read to.

"There are six slices left."

"I'll make us some breakfast."

"Thank you."

Some small part of Martin had been half convinced that Arthur was addressing his cup of tea when he muttered the words, "I love you." He had known how Arthur felt about him for some time now. Known it through a thousand kind actions that Arthur didn't always understand. Known it through patience that few others had ever had for him. Martin had tried to say the words himself before being sent on that disastrous assignment, but they were still too new and there was still too much of himself he had yet to show Arthur, too much he still had to try to explain.

And after, Arthur had given those words back to him and there was no more that needed to be said. And yet, half delirious with exhaustion muttering into a cup of tea, when Arthur said "I love you" Martin jerked as if he'd been struck in the sternum, and for a moment his very breath faltered. He stepped out of the cubicle quickly and returned to his own work with as much focus as he could manage.

His sleep that night was restless and, in the end, he decided to simply read while Arthur caught up on his own rest. Then Arthur had woken up and said those words again. This time it was not a blow. Instead, a warmth seemed to begin in that spot and spread through his body. He knew society expected him to say those words back, but linking the exact words with the right emotions had never been his strong suit.

He'd squeezed Arthur's hand and Arthur got up and made bacon, perfectly even and crispy. Apparently, it requires cooking it a long time on a lower heat.

"I am finalizing my plans for the holidays. Would you still like to join me in New York?"

Arthur smiled. "If you're willing to have me tag along."

"I would... I would enjoy that very much." His annual trip to New York consisted of a day spent in his lawyer's office and a second day attending to some personal matters. Occasionally a third day buying art. Before that, before the Agency, his explorations of what might loosely be described as his home city were limited primarily to school field trips. "Is there anywhere in particular you'd like to see?"

"Oh, I've got a list of 50 restaurants that have two-year long reservation lists which I can't afford, but the Met, that would be a nice start. Central Park. I sort of want to ice skate at Rockefeller Center, just to say I did."

"I do not know how to ice skate."

"I can show you if you like."

Martin tried to picture them gliding over ice together. "That sounds... interesting."

"After spending Christmas with his mother, Arthur will be joining me in New York for a week."

Dr. Francis smiled, bright and honest. She never tried to hide or school her emotions. If anything, Martin thought she might even be telegraphing them a bit for his sake. "That's wonderful."

"He wants to teach me how to ice skate."

"That sounds like fun. Mind your bad leg, however."

"I will."

"Are the two of you going to exchange gifts?"

Martin sighed. He knew he was forgetting something.

Chapter Six

ARTHUR'S BAGS WERE PACKED. He was not ready to go. He had an early flight in the morning but there were reasons he didn't go home for Christmas most years and he had no idea if this year would be better or worse. No uncomfortable, passive-aggressive Christmas dinner between his parents, but also his father wouldn't be there to take the brunt of his mother's anger when he went to see his sisters. And, well, his father wouldn't be there. He wasn't sure how he would feel when he noticed there was no smell of cheap cigarettes lingering in the backyard, no one slipping rum into his coffee. The funeral had been different; it was all too fast, there was too much to do, no time to think or dwell on things. This would just be Christmas.

He wiped dry the last dinner plate and handed it to Martin to put away. No point in running the dishwasher with only the two of them, and there was something about the quiet final chore of the day that Arthur found settling.

Once that was done, Arthur reached into a drawer that was usually empty and pulled out a lumpy package wrapped in green paper.

"I know we didn't really talk about gifts or anything. I mean I don't even know if you do holidays or what religion you are, if any-"

"Technically, Brotherhood of the Third Coming under the Lessons of the Reverend Brown, Ascended."

"Umm..." Arthur's brain froze up. He could feel the giant Program Not Responding error message due to the pure amount of question overload.

Martin shrugged. "Nonpracticing."

"Right." Arthur decided that the five million questions he suddenly had could wait for later and shoved the package into Martin's hands. "Merry Christmas. I mean I know it's not Christmas yet but since I'm going out of town..."

Martin turned the package around in his hands. "May I open it?"

"Please."

Martin neatly picked at the tape, carefully preserving the paper, then unrolled the sturdy fabric inside. The rows of knives gleamed, sharp and new. The handles were mismatched since no one company did every type of knife perfectly, despite what they may advertise, but Arthur had spent a day carefully picking each one.

"You're getting pretty good in the kitchen but your knife, singular, one solitary sharpish blade you own, is not fit for *any* purpose. It's time you have your own set."

Martin smiled at him and ran his finger along the handle of the paring knife. "Thank you." He rolled the blades back up and left the room, returning a minute later with a small package, wrapped in brown paper and twine. He carefully handed it to Arthur and Arthur couldn't help but feel that the package contained a great treasure. He almost dreaded opening it.

He sat down at the table and placed the package neatly in front of him.

The hemp fibers caught as he slowly pulled the ends of the bow, the brown wrapping paper falling easily away. Arthur's hands began to shake, and his breath caught in his lungs. The book was small and the dust jacket a faded yellowed brown, but the text was still clear: *Apicius Cookery and Dining in Imperial Rome. Now for the First Time*

Rendered Into English. At the bottom of the cover, below a print of half-naked Romans feasting, was the date: 1936.

Arthur wanted to tell himself that this was a reprint or clever copy, but he could smell the age of the paper and see the uneven aging of light and handling. And he knew Martin. He swallowed hard. The recipes in the book were almost two thousand years old and only translated for public consumption in the 1930s. The crasser part of his mind wanted to know where Martin could have possibly found it. His mother's thrifty instinct wanted to refuse it for the hundreds of dollars it must have cost, even if he was pretty sure Martin could afford it as he never spent money on anything else.

He reached out to open it but found his hands were still shaking. He clenched them together and took a long breath. "It's beautiful." He tore his eyes from the book and up to Martin's face. "Thank you."

Martin's features relaxed and Arthur began to relax in turn. Flexing his hands, he got the shaking under control and opened the book to a random page. "Green beans," he read "Are cooked in broth, with oil, green coriander, cumin, and chopped leeks, and served."

"Sounds nice."

"I've never done green beans with leeks." A bit of warmth and calm began to override the stress and worry. "We can try it when we get home."

It was always a bit of a surprise for Arthur when his key slid into the lock of his parent's front door. In all the years since he'd left for college, he'd figured there would have been a need to have them replaced at least once. A break-in, a jam, missing keys, something. The key clicked into place and turned smoothly.

"Mom," Arthur called out. The heavy scents of sugar and melted butter swirled thickly through the air.

While Hanh could cook circles around his mother 364 days a year, there was one thing Faith Dram could do above anyone else and that was baking Christmas cookies. And she was a machine. He had hoped to plan his arrival for after the worst of it, but by the smell of things, she was right in the thick of the madness.

"In the kitchen, sweetie!" Her voice rang out across the house.

Arthur put his bags by the door and followed his nose. In the kitchen he found his mother standing there, smiling in her red and green apron, flour on her hands and a smudge of molasses on her cheek mingling with a fine sheen of sweat. The image slapped him with such strong memories he nearly lost his balance.

She smiled at him. "Oh, dear lord, it is so good to see you. How was the flight? I'd give you a hug, but I'm covered in flour."

Arthur pulled his mom close, not caring about the transfer of ingredients. He'd be covered himself soon enough. "The flight was fine. It's good to see you, too," he said, not yet letting go of the hug.

There was the ding of a timer, and his mother began to pull away.

"Don't worry, I'll get it."

Arthur started at the deep masculine voice coming from the breakfast nook. His mother pulled away.

"Arthur, you know David?"

No, he did not know *David*. He knew Coach Edwards who made him run laps in the rain while wearing thin cotton gym clothes and screamed at him until he could do one sorry backwards fling over the high jump bar and made it very clear that he would never be part of any school sports team and therefore was locked out of the upper echelons of the school's social hierarchy. Not to mention the fucking PACER test. He still wasn't sure why the school or government or whoever cared how long and fast he could run.

He held out his hand, using every bit of training to keep it steady, and looked Coach Edwards dead in the eye.

I'm a fucking spy and you can never fuck with me ever again.

The handshake was short and firm before David turned and took a sheet of shortbread cookies from the oven. Arthur gave a quick questioning glance to his mother while his back was turned.

"I was talking to David the other day after church and it turned out he'd never baked a cookie."

No shit. He was very clear about what he thought of boys who took home-ec.

"And then, well, it seems like I'm making more every year," his mother continued. "And he kindly offered to help."

"That's so nice." Arthur watched Coach Edwards try to move sticks of shortbread onto a cooling rack. Yeah, there was only one reason a guy like that offered to help a woman like his mother bake 500 Christmas cookies. The question was whether his mother knew. It wasn't like her marriage hadn't been on life support from day one and she certainly deserved someone better in her life than his father had been. The question was whether Coach Edwards was capable of human feelings (Arthur had his doubts about that) or if he was simply looking for a 'proper' woman to look after him in his later years.

"Shortbread has to cool on the pan for five minutes before moving or it will crumble." Arthur tried for the exact same bored and matter-of-fact tone in which he was told he would not even be allowed to try out for the swim team.

"Oh, let me." His mother leapt back into action. She was very detailed in the number of cookies she baked. While there was some margin for error, she also prided herself in consistency and thrift. A box of cookies and fudge for every dear little old lady in church (judgmental old bats, the lot of them, who did nothing but talk about his family behind their backs). A box for every widower and poor bachelor (a combination of dirty, bigoted old men, and a handful of geriatric closet cases). A box for everyone who held position or authority at the church (all unpleasant and judgmental as well). One extra-large box for the soup kitchen and food pantry (which Arthur wouldn't mind except for the air of superiority that surrounded the people who ran it. Arthur was sure they took the cookies home for themselves). He locked his smile in place. This is why he didn't come home for the holidays.

He pushed up his sleeves. "So, have we made the snickerdoodles yet?"

"Oh no. I need you and your steady hands to decorate the sugar cookies while David keeps rolling the molasses cookies."

That explained the slight stickiness of his former coach's handshake. What was worse was he'd now have to eat his favorite Christmas cookie knowing his walking high school nightmare had his hands all over them.

He kept smiling. "Two hundred filled and frosted Christmas trees coming right up."

Arthur flopped onto the guest bed and stared at his hands. Despite scrubbing, there were speckles of food coloring staining his skin. He knew from hard experience that those were sticking around until at least Christmas day. He'd been more irritated than shocked when he discovered in high school home-ec that not everyone knows how to make royal icing from scratch or how to pipe and fill for total cover decoration. The 'A' he got from knowing that did help balance out the C in gym that semester. He hated track and field and always would.

Whatever. He'd brought his A game tonight, using tweezers to precisely place silver sugar balls on cookie Christmas trees while his ex-gym teacher was relegated to scoop and roll. There would be more baking tomorrow, then delivering to the old ladies and bachelors. And with any luck, *David* wouldn't be around so he could properly talk to his mother. Or at least talk as much as they were able.

He looked at his phone. The urge to write a long bitchy text to Martin, complaining about his mother's love life, was strong and his fingers hovered over the keys. The problem was that he knew their communications were monitored, and interlinked, especially now that they had filed relationship paperwork. There had been no pushback from human resources but that didn't mean they weren't under increased scrutiny. And he didn't want his juvenile whining attached to Martin's name.

He brought up Carol's number.

My high school gym teacher is trying to date my mother.

Carol texted back the laugh/cry emoji.

I spent the afternoon making Christmas cookies with him.

Want me to put out a hit?

Arthur laughed a little, already feeling better.

You don't have that kind of pull.

Fine. Give me his name and I'll dig up dirt for you.

No. I'm an adult. I'll just threaten to slash his tires like any reasonable male in this god-forsaken town.

So noble. Are you going to ask how the bf is?

Carol knew him a little too well.

I was going to whine at you first. How is he?

He was reading something the size of a phone book and eating what looked like an egg salad sandwich on very white bread.

Arthur smiled while being startled at the surprising amount of relief he felt. He had left a loaf of homemade brioche as well as other assorted foodstuffs in Martin's fridge. While Martin's cooking was improving, his shopping skills were not. Arthur was worried he'd slide back into the apple slices and boiled chicken habit the second his back was turned.

That's good.

Don't worry, I won't let him waste away while you're gone.

I'm not worried.

Liar.

How are you?

I'm fine. You've managed the social minimum. Text your life partner and don't think about your mother's love life.

Thanks. You're the best.

I know.

Arthur flipped over to the Agency's messaging app, which deleted messages seconds after they were read and prevented screen grabs. Arthur didn't like it but the only apps on Martin's phone were the Agency's ones.

Hey, there. How are you doing?

They would only be separated for a week but the ghosts of those brutal months they spent apart still haunted both of them. Arthur stared at his phone. There was a chance Martin would already be asleep and would not answer.

I am well. I had the brioche with egg salad that you left for lunch and the fish for dinner.

How were they?

There was an extended pause. He could picture the look on Martin's face as he formulated his reply. The tiny shifts Arthur had learned to look for as he debated flavor and texture. **I believe I overcooked the fish slightly, but I enjoyed the flavor.**

That was high praise.

Seafood can be tricky, especially in small portions. I'll cook it next time and show you how.

Tomorrow I will make the dumplings you left in the freezer. Are you well?

As well as can be expected. He didn't want to burden Martin, a man with no family as far as he knew, with his far too complicated one. **I'll be fine, though. No need to rush to my rescue.**

I will keep that in mind. Sleep well.

Good night.

Good night.

He watched Martin's final words fade from the screen even as they were transferred to an Agency server buried deep somewhere for analysis.

Martin watched Arthur's final words fade. He had been attempting to sleep but rest was proving elusive. He was halfway through a meditation cycle taught to him by Dr. Francis when his phone pinged. There was only one person who used the Agency's messaging app to talk to him. The Agency itself just called.

He wondered how much Arthur wasn't telling him, not wanting to burden him with family drama.

We'll talk in New York.

He knew he and Arthur spoke little compared to most couples, but even one day of the silence that had enveloped him for years was proving unpleasant. Tomorrow he would call, actually hear Arthur's voice, but for now, tonight, watching those words fade, he thinks they are enough to help lure him into sleep.

Chapter Seven

THERE WERE NO HOT breakfasts on cookie baking days. Arthur hunched over a bowl of cornflakes, his upper back stiff and his eyes feeling gritty from the simple half-day of frosting he'd done before. His mother handed him a cup of coffee before sitting down herself, her posture, as always, perfect. He took a couple more bites of breakfast before deciding to just dive right in.

"So, Mom, you and Coach Edwards?"

"What are you talking about, dear?"

Arthur sighed and sat up a little straighter, feeling his spine crackle as he did. "Please don't play dumb, Mom, you're better than that, you always have been. No guy his age who has spent his life single, living off microwave meals, suddenly swings by to help make Christmas cookies."

His mother took a sip of coffee. Black. No sugar, no cream, hot and harsh, brewed by a Mr. Coffee well past its prime.

Arthur took a long drag of his own coffee. Carol had gotten him hooked on coconut milk in his coffee and the splash of milk-milk now left a funny film on his pallet.

"Look, no one would blame you for *stepping out,* Dad least of all. I mean the guy made high school gym a nightmare and I'll threaten him before leaving town but—"

'It hasn't even been a year since we lost your father," his mother snapped but not as harshly as he expected.

Arthur couldn't stop himself from rolling his eyes. "Mom, no one, and I mean No One would expect you to wait whatever is considered the 'appropriate' amount of time. Hell, no one would blame you for installing a dance floor on Dad's grave-"

"Arthur! Please!"

He sighed and rolled his head around. The pillows in the guest room were particularly flat, so between that and hunching over cookies, his neck was not happy with him either.

"Okay, fine, it's just you had me way too young and you wasted your fun years on Dad, who was way too old. Please just, just don't fall in with some meathead..." he struggled to find a word that was allowed in the house, "jerk who is only looking for some helpmate to get him through his later years. Get out first. And I don't mean go on a mission or pilgrimage," he added quickly. "Go someplace fun. A real vacation. Disneyland, Paris, New York, Vegas."

"You haven't exactly been to any of those places, either."

"I'm going to New York," he blurted out, defending himself since she did have a point. Arthur had gone from small town to state university to his rust belt Agency posting.

"When?" Her question was oddly sharp.

"In... in a few days."

"For work?" Counter interrogation training was absolutely useless when it came to mothers.

"No. Um... Martin has some things in New York to take care of over the holidays. I mentioned I'd never been, so he offered to tack on a couple of days, play tourist with me. It's not like I don't have vacation days built up."

"I see." There was a strange tone in his mother's voice that he couldn't quite figure out.

"The point is *you* need to get out of the house. Live a little." He tried to turn the conversation back around.

"The cost—"

"You've got Dad's pension and his life insurance." As part of his 'I work in insurance' cover he had made sure his father had two excellent policies. One for his mother and one to cover Hanh and his sisters. "Please, please think about it before diving right into another relationship. Get out of this town and see at least a little of the world."

"I will think about it."

"That's all I'm asking."

His mother took another sip of her coffee.

"And how is Mr. Grove doing?"

"Better," Arthur replied around a mouthful of cornflakes. Martin had been gone a few weeks when his mother had asked for a contact number or address so she could properly thank him for all his help arranging the funeral. Arthur had panicked and spun a story of a bad car accident and a coma. The fact that his eventual injuries had worked for that story did not make Arthur feel any better. "He's still getting migraines, but I haven't seen him on the cane for a while."

"I'll keep him on the church prayer list. Now finish your breakfast. We need to make fudge today."

Because nothing says the holidays like second degree sugar burns.

Arthur smiled. "Yum."

The agonizing burn on the inside of his wrist had settled into a dull but persistent sting. He could handle vast pots of fry oil, gallons of boiling stock, ovens blasting on high, but for some reason whenever he made candy he got burnt. Every, single, time.

He'd long ago developed a technique of popping outside and shoving his arm in the snow until it went numb and then wrapping the burn in wet paper towels and plastic wrap. Completely not what any first aid manual would recommend, but it left him with just a few bits of browned skin that would flake off in a few days.

"Did you find the box?" he heard his mother call from the parlor.

"Yes," he called back.

As he'd been wrapping his arm, she'd casually mentioned that there was a box of his old things in the closet and if he could sort out anything he wanted to keep so she could put the rest in the charity box when they dropped off cookies tomorrow, that would be helpful.

So now, instead of face planting onto the guest bed, or calling Martin, he was faced with a large box of things that looked like they were mostly leftover from high school.

His mother would have automatically dumped anything she found overly offensive, which is why the bags he had packed off to college had been suspiciously heavy.

On the very top was *The Teen Boy's Guide to the Bible* and the *Christian Guide to High School.*

Nope.

He plopped those into the 'to go' pile.

The next level wasn't much better with a stack of yellowing paper. *Why on earth would I want old Honors Government essays?*

He bypassed the donate pile and dumped those right into the trash.

His phone pinged. To most people it would sound like a standard phone, but each of his apps pinged in an ever so slightly different tone and for different reasons. That was his 'personal' email but coming from a work server.

Who in the hell?

He flicked it open. It was from Carol, and it was a background check on Coach Edwards.

Shit.

It wasn't a huge amount. Just what could be dug up by any local police department running a background check or insurance company deciding on a policy. Truth was, Google or Amazon probably had more information about him sitting in a server farm out in California, but it was enough to work with.

He didn't ask how Carol found out Coach Edwards name. The amount of information that people willingly gave up out there made the job of the Agency and similar organizations so much easier. Carol could say 'I ran into a girl from my 8th grade math class', and Arthur would only need a day, if that, to have a list.

He flicked on his messaging app. **You didn't have to but thank you.**

Merry Christmas. Call your bf. He was seeming a little more locked down than usual at lunch. Reading God Created the Integers. Literal doorstop.

Arthur frowned. He had not, in a million years, expected Martin to suddenly buddy up with someone else in the office just because he was out of town, but he had hoped that he wouldn't completely retreat back into himself.

I will. Thanks.

Martin carefully sorted through the school application information he had been able to gather from the children. Some of the essays would need revision. Not necessarily to make them better but to twist them into something closer to what the schools were looking for. A handful of parents had yet to sign the paperwork and he would need to speak with them after the holidays. He would also need to speak to a few teachers who obviously did not appreciate the heights their pupils were capable of. All the schools were dragging their feet on transcripts.

He rubbed at his eyes, his frustration building. He knew going in this would be difficult and, with a few parents he spoke to, it felt more like a rescue op or hostage negotiation, but the fact was those were easier. And he had experience with those. Hostage takers all wanted something. Usually something tangible and obtainable. Parents, families, those worked on emotion, good, bad, or otherwise. There was no prisoner exchange that could be done for a child who wasn't 'technically' being abused or neglected. Just a child stuck in a home or system where they couldn't be a priority.

His phone rang and he snatched it up, not even checking the caller ID, which was foolish and he knew better.

"Hello?"

"Hey, it's me."

A knot of pain that had been building at the base of Martin's neck suddenly vanished and his shoulders slumped a little.

"Hi." He had not realized how much he'd missed the sound of Arthur's voice, a tangible sign of his presence, and was surprised at the slight breathlessness of his own voice. "How are you doing?"

"Eh. My mother has me cleaning out a box of my stuff from high school. I miss you. How are you doing?"

Martin had gone years without anyone inquiring as to the state of his health or emotions in either seriousness or passing. He'd had to learn that when Arthur asked how he was, he meant it with all possible honesty and sincerity. "I miss you as well. I am attempting to put together the school registration packets. However, certain schools, teachers, and parents are proving... frustrating."

"You'll figure it out. You're good at talking people around to things, so I hear."

"Perhaps not as good as I thought I was."

"You'll manage this." Arthur's voice was soft but also reassuring. "I have faith in you."

"I've never heard you speak of faith."

"My relationship with the very concept of faith is complicated, at best, but yes, I have faith in you."

Martin felt an actual blush rise in his cheeks. He honestly couldn't say when the last time that happened was.

"Thank you."

There was a moment of silence from the other end of the line. "I'll see you in less than a week. We'll be in New York together. We'll do stupid tourist stuff."

"I am looking forward to that. Call me tomorrow?"

"Absolutely."

Chapter Eight

"I'VE BEEN THINKING ABOUT Christmas dinner."

Arthur looked up at his mother from where he'd been carefully arranging sugar cookies into piles of tissue.

"And, well, it is just the two of us this year, and I know you don't get a lot of home-cooked meals, but the thought of a whole spread for just two people..."

"I completely understand, Mom." He didn't say that he had home-cooked meals all the time. His own. And he had noted a distinct lack of a twenty-pound ham or ridiculously giant turkey in the fridge. "We can order a turkey pizza and watch a movie."

"Oh, don't be silly. I was thinking of making those baked chicken breasts with rice and greens. You like those, right?"

Arthur hated them. It was one of his mother's go-to one-pan recipes, but she always overcooked the chicken to a rubbery texture in an attempt to get the rice to cook, and the less said about the greens the better. It didn't help that she refused to use anything but salt and pepper for flavoring. Arthur did an excellent version of it using wild rice and cooking it in a two-piece terracotta bake set he had.

"I love it. And if you want to get a frozen apple pie, I promise I will not tell a soul. I'll take that secret to my grave."

His mother made a little piff sound. "Everyone at church uses frozen pie crusts. And half use canned pie filling."

Arthur put a dramatic hand to his chest. "The scandal."

"Last year, Laura Speckler tried to pass off an obviously frozen chocolate pie as homemade for the pie auction. In the end Pastor Cahill was the only one to bid on her pie, out of pity. The rest of us at least have the good grace to rough up the crusts a bit and buy a separate filling."

Arthur held back the smile. There was no trash talk on earth like nice church lady trash talk. Plenty of it had been directed at his family over the years and it used to hurt, but his mother could give back as good as she got, and he'd stopped giving a fuck somewhere around fifteen when he decided he had bigger problems in life than what his mother's social circle thought of him or his father. He placed a decorative lid on a cookie box.

"That's the last one. Have you got the list?"

Faith held up an extensive list of names, written in her tidy hand. "Checked twice."

"Okay, let's go sugar up this town."

Arthur was sure that every holiday he came home the Christmas cookie list had gotten longer.

"And is this Arthur? All grown up?"

I've been all grown up for comfortably over a decade now, you old bat, he thought at his old Sunday school teacher who used to heavily imply that children even conceived out of wedlock were heading to hell, while giving him the side eye. He smiled and held out cookies, using them as a shield to avoid getting his cheeks pinched.

"Look at your boy here, Faith." Arthur winced as the old bachelor who used to run the local tire shop slapped his arm with surprising strength. "Grew up a right looker."

Dude, you still have time to move to some retirement village in California and pick up a forty-year-old boy toy.

He passed over a box of cookies.

"Oh Faith, you have the most kind and Christian soul." Arthur gritted his teeth as he held out a huge box of cookies to Mrs. Havelsten, who had run the soup kitchen for years and was the wife of one of the wealthiest men in town. She didn't need to work (and made sure everyone knew it) and the soup kitchen and food bank was 'her little way of giving back.' Every single time Arthur encountered the woman, he had the urge to sic the IRS on her.

He rolled his neck around and listened to it pop as soon as he and his mother were back in the car. "Who else is on the list?"

"All the rest we can take to the church with us, and it's nearly six already."

Church, right.

Christmas Eve service, which was not nearly as bad as Easter service because the Second Baptist Church of the Plains had never managed to scrape up the money for an air conditioning system that functioned properly, so with the exception of a few years with freak late snow, it was always broiling by Easter. Christmas was simply cold, but you put on layers, sucked it up, and powered through. Everyone talked fast and got out quickly.

"Welcome home Arthur," Pastor Cahill said with a grin and a handshake.

Arthur had to give the guy credit, he refused to believe he'd lost a soul, and always greeted Arthur like he was selling him a used car while signing him up for his third full-body dunking in holy water.

"Pastor."

"And Faith." Pastor Cahill took the box of cookies. "I know I shouldn't ask, but are there ginger snaps?"

"Absolutely."

"You are the kindest of women."

On that point Arthur couldn't argue, except to point out that his mom was usually *too* kind and got stepped on, and when she did stand up, it was usually at just the wrong moment.

"My little bit of joy to spread."

They entered the church as quickly as possible after that, trying to keep a bit of warmth.

They took their usual seats and Arthur took a deep breath. There had always been times in his life when one parent or another was conspicuous in their absence, and he could feel the void of them like a phantom limb, but the last few days had been particularly hard.

Heading back to work within a day of the madness of his father's funeral had perhaps not left him in a state to recognize the void that would never again be filled. Maybe that's why his mother was reaching for Coach Edwards. He had tried to call her more often, email more regularly, but there must have been so many days she spent in the house without even the presence of his father mutely flipping through the paper for company.

He should have visited, taken some vacation time, but Martin had gone missing and he had spiraled, his own grieving cut short and overlaid with a whole different flavor of panic, worry, and grief. A man sat down next to him in the spot he'd left empty. He vaguely recognized the face but couldn't put a name to it. He could recognize the back of Coach Edwards' head a few pews up, even all these years later. Too much time wondering how much trouble he'd get into trying to bounce a basketball off the back of that head.

Pastor Cahill shook the last hand and headed to the pulpit.

Arthur remembered all the prayers, when to stand up and sit down and vaguely sing on key.

He was hungry enough by the time they got home that he gladly took the microwave meal his mother suggested before heading off to bed.

"Sorry it's so late, I had to take my mother to church."

"That's fine. I was still awake."

Arthur frowned. Really, Martin should have been asleep. "Late night at work?"

"No. I have simply found myself restless."

"A change in routine. I'm sorry." Arthur knew the break of routine had left him with his own level of stress and restlessness.

"Don't be. You have your obligations, as we all do, especially this year."

"Yeah. Has that neighbor of yours gotten his place cleaned up yet?"

"I saw some individuals I believe to be his children taking out bags yesterday. They did not look happy, but neither did he."

"How about those completely bonkers Christmas lights on the other side of the hall? Any headaches?"

He heard Martin take a deep breath. "This morning, I knocked on their door and explained my situation and asked if they could put them on a less frantic pattern."

Arthur sat up. Martin asking for help was damn near unheard of; asking a stranger to change something that was bothering him just might count as a Christmas miracle.

"And?"

"They were understanding. The lights are now on a slowly shifting pattern that is almost soothing."

"Good." He didn't say *I am so unbelievably fucking proud of you for standing up for your own needs and health,*' because that was likely to come across as patronizing, but it didn't change the fact that he was. "I was worried about that."

"I have taken to keeping my medication on me at all times. Just in case."

"That's sensible. I should let you try to sleep."

"You, as well."

"No." Arthur flopped back down on his bed. "I need to stay awake then sneak out of the house and join my sisters for midnight mass one more time."

"For a man with Atheist listed on his file, you have a lot of religion in your life."

Arthur sighed. "Tell me about it."

"Are you actually going where I think you're going?"

Arthur froze. He'd been tiptoeing in his stocking feet, dancing over long memorized squeaky floorboards, barely even breathing. In the end, it didn't matter. He was always half sure that his mother had pretended to be asleep on Christmas Eve while his dad snuck him out to midnight mass with Hanh and his sisters. Now he knew for certain.

"Hi, Mom."

His mother made a low sound of anger that seemed to come from deep in her throat that he had never heard before. "How can you possibly—"

"They are my sisters, and this will probably be the last time I will see all of them, or possibly any of them, and they didn't ask for the weird life Dad inflicted on them any more than I did."

"Just because your father went to them doesn't mean you need to."

Arthur understood the anger that had been quietly festering in her heart since the day she tumbled into bed with a charming drunk nearly twenty-five years her senior, but at some point, she needed to take a deep breath and let it go.

He took the deep breath instead and let it out slowly then began to put on his shoes. "Dad had zero use for religion, organized or otherwise, and that is a bold stance to take in this town, but every Christmas Eve he would drag himself to Second Baptist Church of the Plains and shiver through a sermon on salvation that he didn't believe in and didn't believe he deserved, and he would do that for you. And then a few hours later he would drag himself to St. Brendan of the Prairie and suffer through an hour of badly sung hymns because they have *never* managed to get a music director who wasn't tone deaf, and he would do that for her. And that was his yearly penance. So, this year, one last time, I'm going for Dad, because I could never be a good son to both of you at the same time and this is the last chance I've got." He didn't give his mother a chance to answer, just put on his coat and left. He wondered if his key would fit when he got home.

They stood at the bottom steps of St. Brendan of the Prairie shivering slightly, even in overcoats and gloves.

Sonia gave him a hug, squeezing his ribs to the point of pain. "How's your mother? Not furious at you?"

"She's spitting tacks. With Dad gone, she did not pretend to sleep while I tried to sneak out."

"You know you have the most unbelievably perfect excuse to not be here?"

He shrugged. "One more time, for Dad's sake"

"You're a good son."

"I'm a terrible son."

"Mom." A teenager in an ill-fitting suit let out a long whine.

"Say hi to your Uncle Arthur."

"Hey." There was no enthusiasm in it. Arthur didn't blame the kid. He had no idea how involved a grandfather his dad had been and was barely a teenager himself when he first became an uncle. He tried to keep basic contact with his nieces and nephews, to send checks on big events or birthdays, but he knew he was just the weird, white, sort-of-uncle that grandma didn't really like.

Yvette looked him over. "Really?" The word was filled with a lifetime of distaste.

"Last time you'll ever have to see me if you don't want to." He knew that, aside from Sonia, his sisters never really considered him family. And he didn't blame them. It was a fucked-up situation their dad had left them all in.

"Promise."

Arthur held up two fingers "Scouts honor."

Yvette snorted and walked off.

"You were never a scout." Sonia pointed out with a great deal of amusement.

No, but in retrospect, there was one in high school I was really into.

Hanh stopped in front of him. She was in the same black lace dress she wore every year. He'd never asked, but was half sure it came from Vietnam with her. "Why are you here?"

Always to the point. "Dad's not here. I am." He offered his elbow to Hanh the way he'd seen his father do every Christmas Eve. It was one of two consistently romantic things he ever saw his father do. The other was pruning the roses behind the house so they looked like long stem roses when picked. It let his mother put them in the tall vases when company came over.

She looked him over then nodded and placed her hand on his elbow. He walked her up the stairs of the small church, the rest of the family following behind.

Father Lorene shook his hand once they were through the heavy double doors. "Well, I must say you are the last person I expected to see here tonight."

Arthur shrugged. "Christmas miracle?"

The old priest shook a finger at him, but there was no malice in it. They'd made peace long ago. "Hedging your bets, like your father."

"What can I say, I'm in insurance."

Father Lorene shook his head, then shook Hanh's hand while Arthur made his way to their usual pew. It wasn't a large church. Half the size of Second Baptist but with maybe a third of the congregation, on a good day.

The hymns were as out of tune as he remembered and the lessons were pretty much burned into his brain. The flickering of candles was almost hypnotic, but he knew if he started to fall asleep his dad wouldn't be there to elbow him in the ribs. So, he sang along, stayed seated for the communion, and once they were back outside, took off his coat and let a quick blast of frigid air wake him up.

"You okay to drive?" Sonia asked.

Arthur slapped his cheeks and gave his head a quick shake. "I can make the five miles and two turns."

"Okay, well, don't be a stranger bro."

"You, too. Merry Christmas."

"Merry Christmas."

Chapter Nine

THE GREEN GLOW OF the old-fashioned alarm clock told Arthur it was barely past six in the morning and the house was cold. His mother had been asleep when he returned, or was at least pretending to be, so they hadn't spoken. His mom was usually an early riser, especially on Christmas. He sniffed the air, but there was no sign of breakfast.

A small thread of panic crawled up his spine, the thought that maybe something had happened in her sleep, that the last words spoken to each other had been unpleasant ones. Not even a year earlier he had been trying to remember the last conversation he'd had with his father and couldn't. It was probably something about hockey that Arthur had only half-paid attention to.

He hopped up and wrapped a robe around himself to keep warm, then crept down the hall. If his mother was sleeping, he didn't want to wake her. He was too tired himself and he was way past the age of waking up at the crack of dawn to eagerly open Christmas presents and see what Santa left in his stocking.

The door to his mother's bedroom was open a crack, making it possible to peak in without waking her. He couldn't see much, but there was an ever so slight rise and fall of her chest that he could make out in the dim streetlight coming through the window.

Well, I'm awake.

If he was going to smile through a sub-par Christmas dinner, he was going to make a solid Christmas breakfast.

He started by pulling out a pack of bacon, because there was always a pack of bacon, and tossing it into a low pan. Then he found half a bottle of vinegar left over from who knows what and set about descaling the coffee pot. Because there were still a few places in this country where the coffee revolution hadn't arrived, and his home town was one of them.

He had the urge to go all out, make something like eggs Florentine, but there was no spinach and if by some miracle there was thyme in the spice rack, it would almost certainly be dried and flavorless.

There were, however, plenty of leftover baking supplies. Cinnamon swirl pancakes. He checked in the cupboards and cringed at the collection of aluminum and flaky Teflon pots and pans. He made the decision that he was going to stop being nice and start getting her stainless steel for Mother's Day. He could probably enlist Jennine from next door to steal the old stuff.

The first pancake was in the pan when his mother came into the kitchen. She was fully dressed, hair done, light dusting of makeup, just enough to make her look more proper. She sniffed the air.

"What are you making?"

"Cinnamon pancakes and bacon. Pour yourself some coffee."

She did and took a sip. "Did you change the coffee?"

"Descaled the pot." He gave her a kiss on the cheek. "Merry Christmas, Mom. Sit down and let me make you breakfast."

She sat and watched, sipping her coffee. Arthur put in no flourishes but didn't pretend he didn't know exactly what he was doing when he swirled the cinnamon caramel sauce into the batter before flipping the first pancake, revealing a dark brown spiral in the golden cake.

"How do you get them so fluffy?"

His mother had never asked about anything he'd cooked for her, ever. "Whip up the egg whites separately then carefully mix in the yolk, trying to keep as much volume as possible, then very carefully mix that in with the rest of the ingredients that you've already mixed together. They do these pancakes in Japan where they keep the egg whites completely separate. Treat it like a soufflé. They come out three inches tall and take like ten minutes to cook."

He flipped another out of the pan and eyeballed the bacon, deciding it should be perfectly crisp by the time he got another two pancakes done.

"What's in the swirl?"

"Melted butter, brown sugar, and cinnamon. Not exactly healthy. But it's Christmas."

There were no more questions, but he could feel his mother watching. In an odd way it reminded him of Martin watching him cook when he couldn't stand for more than a couple of minutes, but still liked to sit in the kitchen and watch Arthur prepare food. During those times, Arthur would keep a running commentary of what he was doing so Martin could learn even while healing.

He garnished the plates with orange wedges to cut through the sugar and salt and refilled his mother's coffee before sitting down himself.

"This looks lovely. Thank you."

"Absolutely my pleasure."

They opened their gifts after the breakfast dishes were put away.

"It's a French press." It was porcelain and hand-painted with lilies by a rather Bohemian couple who lived in his building. "Does six cups so I thought you could bring it out when it's your turn to host bible study." He knew his mother was never giving up that Mr. Coffee pot for day-to-day brews, but for the subtle status posturing of one's abilities as a hostess, well, it made very nice coffee.

"Thank you, it's beautiful." She handed him a small, wrapped package.

He carefully pulled off the wrapping and his jaw dropped. It was a copy of *Alphaville*, an intensely obscure French science fiction, new wave, neo-noir film from the mid-sixties. And what was more, it was the Criterion edition, which last he checked was out of print. "Where did you find this!?"

His mother smiled. "In the church charity shop. Still in the plastic wrap with a Borders Books price tag on it. I know you like those types of movies so I thought you might enjoy that one."

"I've never actually seen it. I read about it and have been looking for a copy for ages."

His mom positively beamed. "Well, Merry Christmas."

"Merry Christmas, Mom."

It was more a slight crawling sensation along his spine than the halting footsteps that told him someone had stopped at the entrance to his cubicle. It would not be Arthur, who had returned to his childhood home three days earlier. Aside from Arthur and his direct supervisors, no one else had ever come to his cubicle, and his supervisors had only come on three occasions. That said, he had been informed that other agents had 'warmed up' to him after his absence, and while none spoke, he did get more nods as he passed them in the hall.

"Hey, there."

Agent Jones. Carol. Level 3 analyst. Eastern European specialist. Arthur's friend, and lunch companion when they could not share the meal. Girlfriend of Doctor Jennifer Hernandez, PhD, who had once lectured the library children about dinosaurs.

Arthur turned around. "Agent Jones."

"Agent Groves. It's 6:15 on December 25th. Pack up, we're having Christmas dinner together."

"I was not aware you celebrated Christmas."

"I do not, which is why I know every restaurant in this town that is open tonight. Come on, my girlfriend is stuck in Argentina, trying to dig up an entire Neuquenosaurus before her grant money runs out, and your boyfriend is stuck in the same flavor of small-town Middle America hell I ran screaming from. Pack up. You have your choice between Chinese, Thai, and Indian."

Martin contemplated the *offer,* if it could be called that. He had only interacted with Carol with Arthur present. She was intelligent and never attempted to ask probing questions or comment on his habits. His trauma therapist–who in recent months seems to have become more of a general therapist–had been encouraging him to attempt to form other friendships. He had tried to explain how difficult that was, that patterns and routine gave his life order and that other people caused breaks in those patterns that could verge on physically painful.

Carol, he supposed, was vetted in a way. She understood some small pieces of him, even if it was through the lens of Arthur. And, at worst, it was dinner. He had planned to make himself a croque madame using the knives Arthur had given him. He could easily make it his pre-flight lunch before flying to New York in the evening.

He gave a small nod. "Thai." There were no chopsticks involved, though he was improving on that front, and while he did find the flavor combinations of Indian food intriguing, he often ran into textural issues. Noodles he could handle.

Arthur had gotten away with 'helpfully' sautéing the greens in a pan with a little garlic powder, saving them from being boiled to death. The chicken and rice were still overdone but that didn't really matter. He and his mother had spent the day in quiet, mostly reading, sipping hot chocolate because it was Christmas, and listening to the icy wind outside rattle the trees. There was a time the silence would have bothered him; he would have felt forced to make conversation so no one was stuck alone with their thoughts. It didn't bother him anymore. Partly because his own thoughts no longer felt as lonely, not when he knew there was someone out there who seemed to have an understanding of him.

"Tomorrow, if the weather's not too rough, I'm going to go see Dad."

"That's good. We got the headstone up. It's a very nice one. Your Martin helped me pick it."

There was something about the way she said 'your Martin' that gave him both a warm feeling and pricked up his ears. She'd never used quite that turn of phrase before. Had she heard him on his phone calls? He'd sat through the years of sermons on the subject and seen the pamphlets about 'traditional marriage.' And even if he did have the energy within him to explain the details to his mother in a way she would understand... No. It was Christmas, he was running on less than five hours of sleep, he missed Martin, and he wanted to crawl back to bed.

"He's good at helping people through difficult situations. And he's very generous with his time."

His mother nodded. They ate the apple pie, overly sweet, a little synthetic, but warm and calming, and gave her a hug in front of the Christmas tree.

"Merry Christmas."

She squeezed him more tightly than she ever had before and mumbled something into his shirt that he couldn't make out before pulling back. "Merry Christmas."

The Thai restaurant had a plastic silver Christmas tree in the corner, some tinsel strung over the door, and an option of preset menus. Martin and Carol agreed on the Traditional for Two. The waitress noted it down then brought them their drinks.

Carol raised her glass of sparkling wine and Martin raised his of sparkling water.

"Happy, whatever you might celebrate."

Martin briefly tried to remember the old prayers recited diligently over every meal. "Thank you. Happy Hanukkah, a trifle late," he replied.

Carol smiled. "Thanks."

Martin sipped his water. Alcohol did not mix with several medications he still took, and he was worried about triggering a migraine with Arthur not around. The aggressively twinkling Christmas lights his neighbors had put around their door were bad enough to have him reaching for his dark glasses and fumbling into his apartment nearly blind, at least until he had gathered up the confidence to knock on their door.

Carol sipped her wine. Martin felt his pulse increase slightly, followed by an increase in his respiratory rate. When he had accepted the dinner invitation, he had considered the possibility of small talk, but now that it was in front of him it felt far more unpleasant.

Arthur understood that he didn't talk, that some days he simply couldn't talk, that forcing communication beyond the absolute necessary was too much. It was the same as touch. Some days, Arthur spooned against his back brought him to the edge of pure peace. Other days, even the lightest brush of fingers was more than he could manage, feeling like electrified sandpaper.

A part of him had very much wanted to join Arthur for the holidays, but that would have been unlikely to end well. Slipping in as a kindly face and a helping hand during a time of tragedy had been easy enough. People were distracted. His name was real but everything else a complete fabrication. People were happy for the assistance, and no one looked too closely. Grief and shock had masked the flimsy lies and sub-par acting. The Agency had trained him as best as they were able, but a truly believable performance requires an x factor that he lacked. 'Not everyone is destined for Broadway, or undercover work' his training agent had said with a sigh. Martin had learned enough not to mention that he technically owned two buildings on Broadway.

Christmas would have been far harder to justify. Tricky to keep up the act.

Carol smiled at him. "You don't have to make random conversation. I mostly just didn't want to be sitting here alone. And there may have been a request from someone to make sure you eat a bit tonight."

Martin allowed himself a small smile. Arthur slipping him food was nearly the foundation of their relationship, or at least the starting point.

"It'll probably take another couple of months to get that Neuquenosaurus up and out of the ground, but Jennifer says she'd love to come and talk with your library kids as soon as she's back."

"They will enjoy that."

"She said they asked better questions and wrote more coherent essays than most of the grad students she's lectured."

"I should hope so." Martin had put considerable time into making sure his library children knew how to ask questions that would garner the maximum information. And he did not allow for sloppy reports from them, either.

"Oh, and while Mr. Restaurant isn't here, the best stuffing you can have: make fresh challah bread, cut it into little cubes, toast it in the oven with rosemary infused olive oil and a bit of garlic until it's all nice and crunchy, then shove it up the turkey with a bunch of diced green apple, sage, onion, and a pinch of salt. Absolutely perfect."

Martin nodded. "If I am ever in a position where I have to stuff a turkey, I will keep that in mind."

Chapter Ten

ARTHUR WAS USED TO the cold. He'd grown up in these bitter winters, but that didn't mean he ever liked them. Faded grass, brittle with ice, crunched under his feet as he marched up the hill of the cemetery. He couldn't actually remember what had been picked out for his father's headstone. Those few days were all a little blurry. He did have a vague memory of steering his mother away from having anything overtly religious carved into it.

He stopped at the top of the hill and looked back at the view his dad would not have given a shit about, then down at the stone laid neatly into the grass. It had his father's name and dates. The words Son, Father, and Husband. At the bottom was also his old army unit. That must have been his mother's addition when he wasn't paying attention. A battered little flag was stuck in the earth by the headstone. It looked like it had been there since Veterans Day, probably courtesy of the local VA.

He took a deep breath, and then another. He was alone and cold and let the grief and anger fill him. There was no reason not to. There was no one to be strong for or put on a performance for. The feelings that he had stomped on or simply ignored for months rose up and tried to choke him. Well, here he had it, a moment to *feel*. He let out a single choked sob and finally felt himself begin to settle.

"Hi, Dad." He felt stupid talking to a patch of grass and a smooth lump of rock. "I... I miss you, I guess. It's Christmas. Checked in on Mom. You know how I always said Coach Edwards would look her over in church? Well, guess who just so happened to stop by to 'help' make Christmas cookies." Arthur made little air quotes with his fingers and felt incredibly stupid. "Not like you care because you are dead and can't hear a word I'm saying and I'm only talking to frozen grass."

He closed his eyes and tilted his head back to the gray sky. "Checked in on Hanh and the girls as well. Yvette still hates me. Your grandkids look healthy. I even went to midnight mass and got Mom fucking pissed at me so you're welcome there."

He pulled a bottle of beer out of his deep winter coat pocket, popped off the top, and took a large swig.

"You know how you were always asking me if I had someone special? Well, I do now. He was actually at your funeral. His name is Martin. He's a secret agent and so am I, by the way." Arthur giggled a little to himself and took another sip of beer. "I love him. Took me forever to tell him that. I should tell him every day, but I didn't exactly have much of a role model on that front. Doing my best, though."

Arthur sat down, knowing all he would get was wet pants and a numb ass.

"I came so close to losing him before I even had a chance to tell him... anything. He calms the parts of my brain that always seem to be spinning too fast and in the wrong direction. He fills up the bits of me that I didn't know were empty. And if that isn't the fucking sappiest shit ever to come out of my mouth. Doesn't matter though because you are dead and there is no one listening but the grass."

Arthur took a final sip of beer before emptying the rest of it over the grave in front of him.

"Merry Christmas, Dad."

Martin tipped the driver of the town car generously, even though it was not strictly necessary. He was on retainer with the law firm that managed his holdings and was well paid. Still, a request to drive slowly and gently was not the usual one, especially around the holidays, but the physical sensory pressure of New York City took adjustment that neither the subways nor a standard cab ride provided. The driver took the fifty. "Merry Christmas."

"Happy New Year."

The driver smiled and Martin worked on his smile back. The doorman took his luggage. His nice suits would be waiting in his room. Maybe he should have postponed the trip for a few days and asked Arthur to join him from the start. He'd set his arrival for the middle of the night to lower the potential of a migraine, and his lawyer arranged things so he'd have to interact with as few people as possible.

He was given his room key and stepped into the waiting elevator that whisked him smoothly high into the cold winter night and high above the streets that were still whispering at this late hour. The doors opened directly into the penthouse. He wanted to fall instantly into bed, but he could feel the grime of air travel on his skin. Since the 'incident,' as it was officially called, where he'd been left for months in filth, he'd found himself particularly sensitive to being dirty. Not quite enough for it to count as a full trigger, but less tolerable than it had been.

When he was fully cleaned and changed, he found sleep would not come, despite exhaustion pricking at the edges of his mind.

Breathe. He brought Arthur's voice to mind. *Close your eyes and breathe.* Five counts in, seven out. *I'm here.* Except he wasn't.

He picked up his phone.

I have arrived in New York.

It was late where Arthur was. He would be asleep or should be. His phone pinged one minute later.

Good. Miss you. See you soon.

Martin closed his eyes and slept.

"Mr. Abram." Martin held out his hand. His lawyer stared at it for a second before taking it and engaging in a brief handshake. It wasn't that Martin disliked shaking hands, although there were some days where the touch of another person's skin did make him shudder, but on days that weren't like those, shaking hands was something he simply forgot about until there was an empty hand in front of him and an awkward silence.

"I have known you since you were 10 years old and have *officially* been your lawyer since you were sixteen and I do believe that is the first time we have ever shaken hands."

"I've been working on some things." It was more like undoing. He'd spent years forcing a high level of self-discipline on himself. Hiding every twitch or flinch or fearful glance at the nearest door until he'd gone a bit too far, locked himself a bit too tight. The Agency didn't care if he forgot to smile or shake hands as long as he kept a perfect list of active counter agents in his head, but for his future plans he'd have to loosen up a bit, keep people more at ease. So, every Thursday night, social skills with his therapist. On many levels, the trauma therapy was easier.

Martin sat down and Mr. Abram followed. The hard leather chair with brass studs that Mr. Abram's predecessor had sat in like a throne had been traded out for a contraption made of mesh and plastic that was probably designed for optimized ergonomics.

"So, when did you get married and adopt thirty children?"

"That did not occur and is an exaggeration."

"No, but going by these changes you want made to your trust, will, and various assets, it sure is easy to believe that. So, who is this Arthur?"

"My friend."

"Don't lie to your lawyer."

"He-"

Is the name I put on form B-837.

"Is someone who accepts me exactly as I am and has my heart for it."

Mr. Abram dramatically put a hand to his chest. "Well, that very nearly melts the ball of ice that is my little lawyer heart. Do I get to meet him?"

"Why would you want to?" Martin asked. He was sure it was not legally necessary.

"You don't have family."

"I am aware."

Mr. Abram sighed and pinched the bridge of his nose for a second. "Your aunt's husband was a stone-cold bastard and I was too young, ambitious, and too far down the totem pole to care about the damage he was doing. Then I had to watch your aunt destroy herself and there was nothing I could do about that either. And after that, when you sat in this office and I laid out the empire you had just inherited, you didn't say a word except to ask if you could go back to school. Not the response most of the trust fund Manhattan brats I deal with would have given me. And then after Alice..." Mr. Abram fell silent for a moment before taking a deep breath. "I have been managing that empire for you while you went off and did... something. Now you waltz back in shaking hands and putting a bunch of kids and some guy I've never met on your paperwork. Yeah, I want to meet him."

"Did you love my aunt?" It was something he always wondered. Something about the way Mr. Abram's voice always changed slightly when mentioning her.

"That was your takeaway? I was fond of your aunt. I had a greater fondness for my law license and my job as a junior associate when I met her."

Martin had few detailed memories of his aunt, despite living with her for several years. "She was beautiful, I think."

"She was stunning. And when she was sober, she was funny, intelligent, and caring."

"I don't remember that."

"You wouldn't have." There was a silence that hung between them for a long moment. "Okay, you don't want to talk about the boyfriend, let's talk about the kids."

That was easier. He took from his bag a large collection of file folders.

"Assuming the annual statements are correct and no one has been taking funds without my knowledge, I should have no problem paying the tuition to the selected schools."

"Okay. However, I see two problems. One, you have to get them into the schools; and two, their parents need to sign off on it."

"I am working on the second one. I calculated necessary school 'donations' into the first."

"You're going to bribe them in?"

"It should not be necessary as all excel academically, but you may recall when I started at Trinity, I was only marginally literate and still found electricity deeply suspicious. Considering you were writing the tuition checks, I assumed you smoothed out the application process."

Mr. Abram let out a particularly long sigh. "You'll still need parental permission, and you won't be able to do what I did."

"And what did you do?"

"Put the form in the middle of a bunch of other stuff your aunt needed to sign and that I knew she wouldn't read because she was already self-medicating pretty heavily by then."

"I will handle it." Some of the parents had already signed, leaping at the chance to send their children into the possibility of a brighter future to break the cycle of 80-hour minimum wage work weeks. There were others who were deeply suspicious and would need careful handling to convince. And there were a few who would gladly sign just to have one less mouth to feed.

"Okay. If you can make it happen, I'll make sure the money is there. I mean, you've got enough to do this ten times over."

"With any luck, that is precisely what I will do."

"Can't take it with you?"

"Something like that."

"Now, before we get into signing all the stuff that needs to be signed for the year, I have something for you." Mr. Abram put the children's files to the side, opened a desk drawer and pulled out a standard white envelope with a handwritten address. "It's for you. Arrived 'care of' about three months ago. Considering everything, I've debated even giving it to you. I know I need to but..."

Martin turned the envelope around in his hands. There was no return address. "What does it contain?"

"That... That farm, cult, whatever your mom was a member of, one of the kids is trying to track everyone down. I did some digging and they're legit." Martin felt a tremble start in his hands. "All these years, I know it's probably the one thing we never really covered—"

"Why?" Martin managed to force the word out, but he could feel his throat already tightening.

"I don't know. I made contact, but they only want to speak to you. I did do a bit of snooping and there is currently a property dispute over the land the farm was on, or rather is still on."

Martin knew what it felt like to get kicked in the chest. The shock of pain, the stuttering of the heart and lungs. He glanced down at himself without control, expecting to see a boot print. "What?" His voice was hardly more than a whisper.

"The buildings are still there. Someone's been renting them out as 'Rustic cabins and farm experience vacation' but I guess the local aquifer goes 90% under the land and there's a push to put in a bottling plant near the local town, but it's tied up in court and water rights people and the EPA are getting involved."

Martin's hands were shaking violently. He opened his mouth to say something, to scream maybe. The thought that the farm was still there, that someone, maybe someone he had known, was still living on it; it was too much. The place where his mother had died, where she was probably buried. Where the police had come in the night, pulling him from his bed in the children's room, asking him questions he didn't understand. It was still there. Nothing came out. He wasn't sure if he was even breathing. His fingers were going numb even as his hands shook beyond any control.

"Shit," he heard Mr. Abram say over the rushing of his pulse. "Shit, shit, I'm sorry."

His eyes dropped. He still couldn't make a sound even though he wanted nothing more than to scream. His eyes fell on the swirl of the desktop wood grain. He followed a knot around and around as it looped back on itself. He felt a warm weight across his shoulders and was marginally aware of the room becoming dim. He felt something heavy, cold, and metal slip into his hands, and he gripped on tight.

Eventually, his breath began to settle and the urge to scream faded. He looked down at his hands. They were flipping the object around without conscience thought. It clicked as he turned it inside out, over and over.

"What is this?" He managed to choke out holding up a strange cube.

"Fidget toy. Infinity cube. My daughter has a dozen of them, they help her calm down."

Martin flipped the strange little cube around in his fingers for a few more minutes focusing on the little clacks and infinite twists.

Mr. Abram put a glass of water in front of him. "Do you want me to call anyone?" His voice was soft and gentle. "This Arthur guy, maybe?"

Martin shook his head. He wanted Arthur by his side more than he could explain in that moment. A simple call would not be enough and would only leave Arthur worrying.

He took breaths as long and deep as he could manage, shifting the soft, heavy blanket that had been draped across his shoulders at some point. Dr. Francis had offered him medication for situations like this, but once you were on medication for anything that wasn't completely physical, your access to certain things at the Agency changed. Not officially, but there was a lot at the Agency that wasn't official.

"I'm sorry. I should have eased you into that letter a little more gently."

Martin shook his head again, before taking a sip of water. "Neither of us could have anticipated an intense physiological response to things that happened decades ago."

"Considering how long I've known you, I should have. How about if I type up a response of 'uninterested' and send it for you?"

"No. I'm... No, let me think about it." He had too many questions. Who? Why? Why now?

"Okay, but don't stress yourself sick over it. You've got a husband and twenty kids to take care of now."

"You are still exaggerating the numbers."

"Only slightly. Drink your water, take your time, it'll be okay."

Chapter Eleven

Arthur squared his shoulders and went into what he called 'secret agent mode.' He'd never actually used it in the course of his job. Mostly it came out when he was arguing over warranties or on the phone with tech support.

He told his mother he was going out for a quick bit of post-Christmas shopping. Which was true, but he had one other stop he needed to make.

He took off his gloves so the knock on the door would be extra sharp and clear. He waited as heavy steps neared the door. There was the click of a lock and the door opened.

"Arthur?"

"Mr. Edwards." Arthur kept his voice as crisp as the winter air.

"Call me David. Come in." He tried to gesture Arthur inside.

"No. I don't think I will. This will only take a moment. I'm just here to remind you that I am in insurance, which means I can find out everything about you."

Coach Edwards looked briefly confused. "I thought you were in industrial insurance or something?"

"Shipping. And insurance is insurance. We were big data when that meant wooden crates and quill pens. We know everything. So, if say, hypothetically, you were pulled over for drunk driving at age twenty, and one of our Hicksville judges let you off on a 'boys will be boys' defense, I could find out about it."

Coach Edwards blanched.

"And if you were picked up in a bar fight at age twenty-three and the judge waved the whole thing as long as you promised to pay for some broken pool cues, well, I might be able to find that out as well."

His face went from white to red. "Now just—"

"No. My mother is very against the evils of alcohol and does not believe in violence. She also has some fairly understandable issues around adultery. And considering the entire school knew about you and the very married Mrs. Fairworth, well..."

"Are you actually trying to blackmail me, boy?" Coach Edwards used the same snarling voice that had once sent Arthur, and hundreds of other boys, sprinting around the school track. It didn't work anymore.

"There is no *trying* here. I am. Now, if you have a genuine fondness for my mother, then I suggest taking a page from the Catholics: confess *all* your sins to her, and repent. If, on the other hand, you are just looking for someone to wipe your ass when your brain melts out your ears in a few years then I *highly* recommend you keep walking. Are we clear?"

Coach Edwards tried to stare him down. It didn't work in the slightest. "Understood."

"Good." Arthur put on his gloves, and with no other comment, walked away.

SIRANG was the note taped above the little button. He would send someone around to fix the doorbell as soon as he could. They had stopped pretending that, through various layers of lawyers and property managers, he wasn't her very generous landlord, but they never spoke of it, and she hated to ask for any repair work or help. One winter he had come and found her trying to fix her own heater while ice formed on the windows.

He stripped off one glove and knocked, then waited. If she was at the market or with a friend, it could be a long wait. It didn't matter. This was the only thing on his schedule until six that evening. He put his glove back on and stuck his hands in his pockets. People scurrying along the sidewalk, dodging patches of ice, looked at him sideways but no one approached.

He heard the snick of the peephole cover. He looked into it. There was the click of various locks being opened and the final rattle of a chain. Tala opened the door. Short and weathered with steel gray hair, she looked him up and down.

"Someone's been feeding you." It was a statement with a heavy undertone of questions. Who? Why?

"Yes." How she could tell under the layers of suits and winter clothes, he didn't know, but then she could tell when anyone was underfed with the same glance. She stepped aside. He stepped in.

The apartment was warm and felt dry. He couldn't hear any pipes clanging. She led him to the small table, only steps from the stove. He could easily put her up in someplace bigger. Let her live in luxury. She would never accept it.

Martin sat.

Tala turned on the stove under a large, heavy pot.

"You are well."

Another statement.

"Yes." In all years past, this was the annual administrative task that he needed to take care of himself or else find someone to take care of it for him. She was one of only two people left alive who had truly known him as he was and seen what he had become.

At the farm, there was the Time of Confession. He had been too young to participate, but he remembered the adults and older children entering the barn every week and exiting in tears. Another six months and he would have joined them.

Tala was his Time of Confession. Not that he confessed anything. She looked at him and knew what needed to be said between small bursts of idle conversation. Even if it was things he didn't want to hear or wouldn't act upon.

She poured thick coffee from a pot into two cups. She placed one in front of him before sitting and sipping the other.

"Are you well?" he asked. She shrugged. This was their conversation. There had been people in his life who judged him for his quiet and people who simply existed in the quiet with him.

"Your sons?"

"Well."

He knew exactly how they were, just as he knew she had been to the doctor two months ago and had a mammogram a month before that.

"Who is feeding you?" she asked.

"I met someone. At work," he added. He didn't want to give her the impression that he'd magically gained the desire to flirt with strangers at a bar.

"Good."

There was no more conversation over the course of several sips of coffee. The lid on the pot began to rattle. She stood and took off the lid, letting a cloud of steam fill the kitchen.

"Chicken stock."

She looked over her shoulder at him. "Yes. Can you cook now, too?" It was teasing, but also a deeper question into the changes in his life.

"A little. I can make a croque madame."

She waved a dismissive hand. "I'll show you how to make sotanghon. Real food."

Tala had been his aunt's housekeeper. An older woman named Diwa had technically been the cook, but the two had worked together. When a terrified and confused child was dumped into the New York penthouse where they worked, they had teamed up to keep him as fed and settled as he could get.

He had spent the last couple of months trying to recreate Diwa's soups, but between his general lack of culinary knowledge and imperfect memory, they were never quite right.

Tala put a cutting board and a large knife with a cracked plastic grip in front of him. "Chop what I tell you to."

Martin only nodded and felt more relaxed than he had since coming to New York.

"I'll send you some pictures from New York," Arthur said as he gave his mother a tight hug.

"Please be safe. It's such a big city and all those people—"

He kissed the side of her head. "I will be fine, I promise."

"I know, but I'm your mother, I get to worry. At least call me when you land so I know the flight went okay."

"Of course."

She pulled him close again. "Are you happy?" Her voice was soft and small, and Arthur almost couldn't make out the words as they were whispered into his shoulder.

"Yes, I am."

"Good," she replied, her voice hardly more than a whisper now. Then she pushed him back to arm's length. "Okay, you've got a flight to catch. Enjoy New York."

He smiled at her, "I'll send you a postcard of something beautiful."

Chapter Twelve

THE LETTER WAS PRINTED on cheap paper and signed in ballpoint blue. As a member of a government security agency, he should be harder to find than this. But as a member of a government security agency, he knew that it was nearly impossible to truly hide if the person looking was motivated enough. And it wasn't as if it had come to his home address. Rather to the estate manager for the properties on which he was listed as the owner.

The farm was only a few hours away. He could start driving and be there by dark. He wouldn't though. Instead, he would pick up Arthur from the airport and they'd go to the hotel. Arthur would probably want to go out somewhere nice for dinner. New York was known for its restaurants, after all. A phone number and email were handwritten under the signature. It had already sat with his attorney for months so there was no need to rush any form of reply. He folded the letter back into its envelope and slid it into his pocket. Maybe it would fall out and he could forget about it.

When Arthur was in high school, he'd read *The Long Dark Tea-Time of the Soul* by Douglas Adams. At the time, he had never been more than fifty miles from his hometown, and Adams' long explanation about why no language on Earth had ever produced the expression "as pretty as an airport" stuck in his head. As he twisted around, looking for the signs or arrows that would point him to where he could find a cab, he wondered if Adams had traveled through LaGuardia prior to writing it.

He was so turned around, he almost walked past the man in the black cap and suit who was holding a sign with the name Arthur Dram written on it. He backtracked and looked at the sign. "That's my name, but I didn't arrange a car."

"Mr. Grove arranged one for you. In fact, he is waiting in the car."

Arthur grinned. "Awesome."

He followed the driver out the door. Some part of him wondered if he was about to be kidnapped, but then his phone pinged.

I have arranged for a driver to pick you up. I am waiting in the car.

He trotted a little to keep up with the driver and was sure to crouch down and peak into the long black town car before getting in.

Martin smiled at him. Arthur crawled in and flopped down onto the thick, wide seat. "Oh, I've missed you."

Martin held out his hand and Arthur took it. "I have missed you, too."

Arthur was sure the lights of New York going by outside the slightly tinted windows were lovely, but he figured he could look at them another night. Right now, he just wanted to look at Martin and feel the tension of the holidays bleed from his system.

Martin had insisted on arranging and covering everything, even though Arthur had tried to help. It had almost become their first fight, but Arthur decided it wasn't worth it. They pulled up to a hotel that looked nice from the outside. A uniformed doorman welcomed them while a bellhop took Arthur's luggage and followed them to the elevator. The elevator whisked them up and Arthur watched the numbers climb, wondering how high they would go. They stopped at the top. Arthur was expecting a hallway, not a foyer. The bellhop placed his luggage on a preset stand. "Will there be anything else you require this evening, Mr. Grove?"

"No. We may go out later, but a turndown service will not be necessary."

"Have a good evening then, Mr. Grove."

Arthur was turning around, his jaw slightly open. This had to be bigger than his and Martin's apartments combined. It was absolutely elegant, without being tacky in any way. Arthur was afraid to touch anything.

"You got us the penthouse suite?" Arthur failed to keep the squeak out of his voice.

"I ask my lawyer to arrange lodging where I will feel the most comfortable."

"And he thinks you'll feel comfortable here?"

"He thinks I will have to interact with the fewest number of random people here."

Arthur thought about that for a moment. "Okay, I can see where that might be coming from. Will you be okay if I try dragging you out to museums and tourist traps? I mean, even at this time of year—"

Martin raised a hand and Arthur fell silent. "You will be with me and I will be fine."

"Okay. If you get overwhelmed or your leg starts hurting, promise you'll tell me and we'll bail on whatever it is."

"I promise."

It was barely past six. Arthur wanted to change out of his travel clothes, wash the airport off him, and dive into the New York food scene. Or at least get pizza.

He was drying off from the shower and digging around his suitcase for some clean socks when Arthur felt the sharp edge of plastic under his fingers and pulled a CD case out from under his underwear. "Oh, I have something for you. My mother found it when she was cleaning out some of my old stuff."

Martin took the case and turned it around in his hands. "A CD?"

"It's a music mix I made in high school. There was this guy I was going to give it to, but he made the football team so..." Arthur gave a little shrug and Martin tilted his head in a way that Arthur knew meant he was completely confused. "At my high school, if you were on the football team, you were royalty and you did not accept mixes from commoners. Especially male ones who were into you, occasionally wore eyeliner, and you used to play Dungeons and Dragons with before ascending to the lofty ranks of 'guys who crashed into each other while trying to chase a ball' and, wow, that came out sounding way more bitter than I intended."

Martin smiled. "Thank you. What music is on it?"

"Honestly, I have zero idea, anymore. Probably some weird combination of Queen, Bowie, Alanis Morissette, with a little Nirvana thrown in. Maybe. Mostly I remember making it while my mother was out of the house because rock and roll is the Devil's Music."

"Is it?"

Now he could tell Martin was laughing at him a little. "Oh, yes. Even Christian Rock. That's the Devil trying to fool you."

Martin shook his head and tucked the CD into his bag. "And how is your mother?"

"Flourishing. Widowhood suits her well. Though my ex-gym teacher is trying to date her. Going to have to keep an eye on that. She's keeping you on the church prayer list until I tell her your migraines have gone away."

"That might be some time yet."

Arthur let it drop. "So, dinner in New York City. Where would you like to go?"

Martin seldom had an opinion about eating meals out and usually seemed happy to let Arthur take the lead on the food front in general, but New York City was his home turf. He must have one restaurant, or deli, or even a hot dog stand that meant home to him.

"You may choose." Martin glanced away and Arthur resisted the urge to sigh. How do you spend any time in a food mecca and have no place you want to eat?

"Great. I want pizza. A guy I used to know told me about this place in Greenwich Village that's supposed to be perfect. You can show me how to ride the subway."

"I have not done that in many years and not often."

"Then it'll be an adventure."

The subway was like nothing Arthur had ever experienced and yet, almost what he expected. Years of books and film describing the process had not fully prepared him for the way he was jostled as he moved too slowly through the line, the slightly sticky feeling of the pole he clung to. The complete incomprehension of the conductor's voice through the crackling speakers. The odd straining of his muscles as he tried to find a way to stand that would not send him crashing into other riders as the train took a sharp turn, showing him as the obvious tourist that he was.

He completely believed all those stories about strange subspecies of bugs and rodents that had evolved to live within the New York subways. Some of the other riders looked like they were their own species as well: pale, eyes down, and moving easily with every jolt and stop. Martin, at his elbow, as well as a thin film of pride, kept him from getting off at whatever the next stop might be and hailing a cab.

He'd done his best to count stops and memorize maps, putting old training to use, but it was Martin's hand gently at the small of his back that gave him the confidence to step onto the platform and not be horribly lost. The dry, crisp, winter air bit, in sharp contrast to the subtropical humidity that the long tunnels managed to maintain. Turning around to find his bearings, he looked up and saw the IFC theater brightly advertising at least three of his favorite noir films.

"Okay, we're coming back here." He hadn't bothered to check what was in the area when he picked dinner and it had absolutely never crossed his mind to look up this particular theater, but he supposed that was New York. A surprise around every corner, something to discover at every stop. He took a deep breath and his stomach growled. "Right, first, pizza."

The pizza was good. Pepperoni and mushrooms for him and tomatoes and peppers for Martin. But what was better, as far as Arthur was concerned, was that it 'felt' like what he imagined a New York pizza place was. The tables were small. The pizza came on paper plates. The walls were covered in layer after layer of faded gig posters. Add in the glimmer of frozen air threatening snow wafting through Greenwich Village and he could believe Simon and Garfunkel sat there to write "Hazy Shade of Winter".

"How's your pizza?"

Martin nodded as he wiped some grease from his lips. "Good."

While it was fun taking Martin on a foodie world tour, he took a certain amount of pride in getting Martin to have preferences in pizza toppings.

"Is there anything in particular you would like to do tomorrow?" Martin asked. "I have cleared my schedule, with the exception of the 30th, when I will have to make two stops. You may join me if you wish or explore the city yourself."

Arthur fully planned to stay glued to Martin's side during this trip for all manner of reasons. "Well, if you're up for it, I was thinking of the Met. Start big right? It *is* New York."

"The Met is big. And a good place to start."

Arthur gave Martin's hand a squeeze before focusing back on his pizza.

After pizza, they strolled through the New York night, letting soft flakes of snow land on their hair. There was no need to rush and the streets were empty enough that their pace would not provoke anyone's ire. Even in the city that never sleeps, things seemed to be spinning down for the night.

Martin watched as Arthur eagerly noted down the location of an all-night diner as well as the upcoming schedule of the theater outside the subway station. He had no doubt they would be returning, judging by the look on Arthur's face.

The ride back was easier. Somehow the rattle and screech of the trains seemed muffled by the snow above.

By the time the elevator was whisking them to the uppermost level of their hotel, he could see Arthur holding back the exhaustion of travel. Martin also had the feeling he hadn't slept well while visiting home.

"Definitely time for bed," Arthur mumbled, stretching out his arms and rolling his neck.

"I agree." As Martin took off his coat, he felt the envelope still in his pocket. It was absurd carrying it around, but for some reason he didn't want to leave it in the room. He shoved it back in, hearing the crackle of the paper, and got ready for bed, looking forward to sleep with the sound of Arthur gently breathing beside him.

Chapter Thirteen

"Now, ARE YOU SURE you don't mind running around playing foodie tourist?" Arthur asked one more time. After sleeping in, they had gotten room service for breakfast, but Arthur was determined that breakfast the next day would be from the deli he saw on the corner. The twitch of Martin's lips, that on others would be a grin, settled Arthur's nerves.

"I did not go out much when I did live here, and I am sure it has changed extensively since I left."

"Tell me if your leg starts to hurt and we'll slow down."

"Of course." In theory, migraines aside, Martin was completely physically healed from his ordeal, but there were still moments late in the day or first thing in the morning when his usually still face would flash with pain and his hand would reach for the nearest solid object seeking support. "I do come here every winter. If we don't see everything, there will be future opportunities."

That thought fluttered across Arthur's mind. They had never talked about how long this thing of theirs might last, but the idea that he wouldn't be here in New York with Martin next winter seemed like an impossible one. Or the winter after that. "I do want to see the Met and from what I've heard that can take a week to go through."

"It can."

"I'd like to at least see the modern and contemporary art section. If you're into that."

"I think that will be a fine place to start."

It took two subway transfers and a stroll to get from their hotel to the front steps of the Met.

Arthur figured as long as he wasn't an *ugly boorish* tourist, he could be a tourist. He craned his neck to take in the vast foyer. Martin had a map but didn't so much as glance at it as he led them into the twisting depths of the museum.

The last time he had been to an art museum with anyone was in university. It had killed that relationship as conflicting opinions on contemporary art can reveal deep incompatibilities. At least in Arthur's case. He wasn't worried this time. They strolled together, stopping occasionally to look at an old master or 60's pop art. He put his hands in his pockets to keep from reaching out and touching the van Gogh that hung on a wall with no guards or velvet rope. It wasn't crowded and he felt no guilt in lingering so he could closely examine paintings he'd only seen in books or as cheap prints.

"I read a surprising percentage of paintings in museums are forgeries, or at least wrongly attributed."

The room of early impressionist masterpieces was empty except for the two of them.

"That one." Martin pointed to a Degas ballet girl. "And that one." He pointed to a Monet haystack in a line with three other haystacks. "The van Goghs are real. They are nearly impossible to forge."

"Seriously?" Arthur swiveled his head between the ballet girl and the haystacks before carefully examining Martin's face for some sign he was being messed with. Despite office rumor to the contrary, Martin did possess a prankster sense of humor. "How can you tell?"

Martin quirked an eyebrow and casually strolled from the gallery, Arthur at his heels. They meandered for another hour. Every so often Martin would point at another painting, almost always within a group of others accredited to the same artist. Arthur still couldn't tell if he was being messed with or if Martin could see some detail that made those stand out against the others.

"Shouldn't you, maybe, tell someone?"

Martin shrugged slightly. "Does knowing the person who applied the paint to the canvas detract from the appreciation of the art or the admiration for the skill?"

Arthur blinked. He did not expect a guy who spent years eating exactly four foods and owning two outfits to have some serious thoughts about art appreciation.

They had lunch at Café Sabarsky and discussed international art forgery and how it pertained to money laundering. They had never discussed the exact details of their work. It wasn't just against policy, but technically illegal. Still, Martin seemed to know exactly how much a quality forged Monet, verses a real one, went for in backrooms five years ago.

"Would you like to go back to the Met?" Martin asked as their plates were cleared away.

"I don't think I could do more of it justice before they closed. Would you be up for strolling around Central Park a little, if it's not too cold for you?"

"I can handle the cold."

Arthur figured it was the speed of their walk through the park that pegged them as tourists, or at least a couple with no deadline and nowhere to be. As New Yorkers rushed by, bundled up against the clear-day cold, Arthur fell out of sync with the surrounding city. He reached out his hand. Arthur didn't fully expect Martin to take it. There were times when he wouldn't or couldn't touch. Sometimes for days and almost never in public. But some days...

Martin's fingers interlaced with his as they crunched along the frozen gravel path and Arthur felt warm and grounded.

They strolled through the park until the light was fading. Arthur turned them towards a hole-in-the-wall noodle shop he'd heard about from some deep part of the foodie Internet.

The noodles were good, but Martin preferred the ones from the shop three blocks from the library back home. He made the decision to hail a cab back to the hotel, not feeling up to navigating the subway again that day.

Arthur was putting away some postcards he'd bought when Martin took out the letter that had spent another day in his pocket.

"You keep looking at that letter; is there anything I can help with?"

"No." Arthur nodded and Martin felt the weight of guilt. He should explain. Arthur had always been open about his past, his complicated family dynamics. And for what he knew of Martin, he had never judged, only waited, letting Martin come to him in his own time. He had told the truth: there was nothing Arthur could do to help since what it was was not technically a problem. Only a decision to be made.

He took a deep breath and put the letter into the envelope, but kept his back turned to Arthur. It would be easier to get out the words if he couldn't see Arthur's reactions. "I was born—" he swallowed a few times and forced his lips to form the right words, the accurate words. "In a cult."

"I'd sort of guessed that." There was no judgment in Arthur's voice and Martin relaxed slightly.

"Yes. I don't have bad memories of it. I remember it as peaceful, quiet, beautiful. I remember my mother loving me. But all my memories are filtered through the lens of childhood. I can't say what might have been going on that I never saw. My mother died when I was ten. I'm not sure of what. Probably something treatable. They told me not to grieve because I would see her after the ascension. I just had to stay with the other children, do as I was told, and be patient."

He took a deep breath. It had taken a long time before he let himself recognize the loss for what it was and longer still before he grieved.

"Not long after she passed, there was a raid of some sort. Child services returned most of us to our mothers, but after two months in foster care, I was sent here to live with an aunt I hadn't known existed." He ran his finger along the edge of the envelope. It reminded him of a silver butter knife that had so confused him with its dull blade and strange shape. "One of the other children is tracking us all down. Wants to speak to all of us."

"Why?"

"I don't know. According to my lawyer, there is currently some controversy over an attempt to tap the aquifer under the land."

"Maybe someone's making a documentary. Those seem to be all the rage."

"I do not think that is something I would feel comfortable participating in."

Arthur stepped slightly behind him and placed his chin gently on Martin shoulder. "If you'd like me to sit in on the call or write a fuck off email for you, I can."

Martin smiled. "My lawyer made a very similar offer. I am... I had a panic attack when he told me the farm even still existed. It's apparently a bed and breakfast now."

"What?" Arthur stepped in front of him. "Why didn't you tell me?"

"I didn't want you to worry, and there was nothing you could have done. Mr. Abram has known me since I was ten and his own child is prone to... heightened emotional distress. He was able to... help."

Arthur pinched his lips tight for a moment. "I still wish you'd have told me. I'd rather know and be worried than kept in the dark." Martin nodded, a little thread of guilt coming up. "But I'm glad you told me now." Arthur took the envelope from his hands and placed it on the small desk. "Come on, you said you had some stuff to handle tomorrow, so let's both get some rest."

"Yes. It might be a long day."

Chapter Fourteen

THE CHOLESTEROL OF A proper New York deli bacon egg and cheese sandwich was settling into Arthur's arteries, but he had always had a strange working theory that it could be washed out with enough black coffee. Martin's breakfast was a simple bagel and cream cheese, but the cream cheese was layered on so thick there was possibly more cheese than bagel. He was eating it with fastidious small bites. The previous day, he had dressed the way he normally dressed for the library with the simple addition of a warmer coat. Today he was in a full suit and not one of his standard work suits. This looked tailor-made and seemed designed to project power and wealth.

"So, where are we heading?" Arthur asked between sips of black, almost tar-like coffee, that he would normally turn his nose up at, but like with so many dining experiences, setting and context is everything.

"I have to swing by the library, then go shopping."

Martin led them up the fine marble steps of the New York Public Library and past the grand lions that Arthur had only seen in movies. As they passed through the front doors, they were approached by a middle-aged woman with short cropped hair in a dark blue business suit.

"Mister Grove, a pleasure to see you again." The woman had her hands clasped behind her back and nodded politely.

"You as well. This is Arthur Dram. Arthur, this is archival acquisitions director Doctor Abigale York."

"Pleasure," Arthur also nodded in greeting.

"Shall we?" Dr. York asked.

"Of course."

Dr. York turned and began to walk briskly through the library. Martin seemed to know exactly where he was going as he followed. Meanwhile, Arthur craned his neck up, trying to make out the details of the painted ceiling while flicking his head around to take in the carvings and the wood and marble. And if he had had a VHS of Ghostbusters as a kid that he hid from his mother and watched way too many times, and in retrospect might have had a crush on Egon, well he didn't care if that showed on his face.

He trotted a little to keep up with Martin and their guide. They went through heavy wooden doors, and down small hallways until they reached a set of doors labeled with things like "Rare Collection" and "Authorized Guests Only." They were swiped into a small room. In the middle of the room was a table with two chairs. A single, small, leather-bound book was waiting.

"I must say, I was surprised at the suggestion, but a piece like this is seldom on the open market and of course with your donation—"

Martin waved a dismissive hand before sitting and gently opening the text. He motioned Arthur to sit at the other chair.

"Fifteenth century, hand-copied and illuminated," Dr. York supplied.

Arthur couldn't see what the text was, but his eyes went wide at the date. "Shouldn't we be wearing gloves or masks or something?"

Martin glanced at him briefly while continuing to turn pages.

"Fibers, chemicals, and decreased dexterity would risk far more damage than a little skin oil" Dr. York replied patiently. "This is parchment, not wood pulp paper. Completely different material."

Martin looked at him again. "*Le Viandier de Taillevent.*"

For a moment Arthur's heart stopped and he was glad he was already sitting. Martin gently pushed the book towards him. A collection of French recipes from the thirteen hundreds. Practically the invention of *haute cuisine*. He raised his hand to touch it but found it shaking and quickly slammed it down into his lap.

"It will be scanned and added to the digital collection."

Arthur took long deep breaths, trying to remember his standard training from the Agency. Once his hands stopped shaking, he carefully reached out and turned a page that was dry, but not brittle. The ink looked surprisingly fresh.

"I wish I could read this. I mean, I have it in English and modern French but..."

He slowly turned the pages. Illustrations of ingredients, equipment, and kitchen layout nearly danced from still bright inks. Then he stopped and a smile stretched across his face. There was a smudge, not in the ink or the illustrations, but over it, light brown and faded.

"What is it?" Martin asked.

"Gravy. Maybe a wine sauce." He pointed with his pinky. "This book sat in a kitchen. Some working cook looked over this page to check something and dropped gravy or sauce, maybe broth but it looks too thick. Probably said 'merde' and tried to wipe it away. This was a working book. Books like this should be. You could probably shake flour out from between some pages. Makes me happy."

Martin gave one of his small fond smiles.

"I'll have that noted when it's digitized. The conservators might want to look for traces of grain or protein."

Arthur closed the book and put his hands in his lap again, mostly to resist the urge to grab the book and make a run for it.

"Would you care to see the other purchases?" Dr. York asked.

"That will not be necessary. Thank you," Martin replied as he stood.

Arthur stood as well but had a hard time ripping his eyes away from the small book on the table.

"In that case, would you like to see the renovations? They should be fully completed by February but are already in use."

"Thank you. Yes."

Arthur followed along as they were once again led through twists and turns until they were back in the public area and ushered through a door marked Children's Room. Kids were curled up in beanbag chairs and parents helped others look over the shelves. Dr. York led them to the far end of the room and around the corner.

What Arthur saw looked achingly familiar and at the same time newer, and more modern. The paint smell was still lingering. "We are, of course, keeping up the children's story hour. We have also hired three staff who are currently working towards their master's degrees in education to provide homework help to any child who needs it. Three until closing."

"Excellent."

Arthur ghosted his fingers across a box labeled 'quote of the day.' It was carved of a deep red wood. The one in their library at home was brightly colored and made of popsicle sticks and an old tissue box. He wondered if their story hour reader could get through *Beowulf* in old English. Probably not.

Martin sat in the adult-sized chair, obviously meant for their reader. He looked out of place in a way he didn't back home, and Arthur could see the smallest signs of stress twitch around his eyes. He wondered how much Martin had left to do if he was stressed already.

"Is there anything else I can help you with, Mr. Grove?" Dr. York asked.

Martin shook his head. "No. Thank you. I can show myself out."

Arthur waited for Dr. York to leave before approaching Martin, who had closed his eyes and was breathing slowly. "It's warm in here. Why don't we step outside, get some fresh-ish air?"

Martin nodded and got up, leading Arthur from the library.

The stone of the lion was cold under his hands, but he left his gloves in his pocket. He let the smooth marble stir his memories. He sat on one of the lower steps, well aware of what New Yorkers tracked on their shoes and the value of his suit and coat. Arthur sat next to him a moment later.

"So, being friends with librarians isn't a new thing."

Martin held out his hand, palm up. There were things he needed to explain, actually wanted to tell, stories and explanations that had never crossed his lips and now seemed determined to choke him if they could not spill out. Things he needed to explain especially if... He knew Mr. Abram had been teasing him when he said he had gotten married and adopted twenty children. He was one of the only people who could tease him, softly and gently, and yet the idea of Arthur *not* being with him in New York the next winter or any winter after was not a tolerable one, and his mind, usually so able to focus, skittered away from that idea. But he was sure that for that to happen, Arthur needed to know the many truths he'd buried under silence and solitude.

Arthur gently laid his hand in Martin's and gave it a squeeze. Martin visualized the warmth of Arthur's hand and pictured bringing it into himself. He took long slow breaths, the way his therapist had taught him.

"The first time I came here, I was running away. I was terrified and ran from my aunt's apartment blindly into the streets. I didn't understand anything. It was so noisy and the air was so thick I could hardly breathe. When I passed here, it was the grandest building I had seen, so I thought it was a Gathering Hall. I had no other frame of reference. One of the librarians found me walking around. She spoke soft and slow and I think I started to cry. I'd only ever really seen a few proper books in my life. I'd only known about electricity for a couple of months. She let me calm down in the children's section before calling the police."

Arthur squeezed his hand again. Martin glanced over and could tell he had questions but was also not asking them, letting Martin take his time.

"The police didn't notice or didn't care about my aunt's intoxication when they brought me back. I described this place to our housekeeper. I didn't even know the word library. She walked me back the next day and I memorized how to get here. I came every day until someone realized they should probably sign me up for school. Not that that went well."

Martin looked up from their joined hands to Arthur's face, he could see the questions forming, and dots being connected.

Martin took a deep breath and stood up. "Would you be willing to come with me while I make a purchase?"

Arthur blinked a few times at the sudden change of topics. "Sure. I've been dragging you around playing tourist. What are you getting?"

"Art."

Chapter Fifteen

THE VISCERAL FEAR WAS threatening to paralyze Martin as he stepped out of the town car, despite having done this a dozen times before. He understood why. There was logic behind the trembling in his fingers. He knew in agonizing detail what exactly had changed between the last time he had to meet some shady characters and this time, but that did not change the fact that he already wanted to vomit. He had hoped having Arthur present would make things easier.

Mostly he wished he could send someone else to do this, but he was the only one; he had to see each piece for himself to be truly sure.

Arthur looked more curious than anything when they were dropped in front of a once grand hotel in what was now an unsavory neighborhood. The man at the desk hadn't even looked up as they walked past and ascended creaking stairs with threadbare carpet that had once been red.

Martin knocked on the door of room 301.

"How above board is this?" Arthur asked quietly.

"I am merely reclaiming what is rightfully mine."

"That is not a comforting answer."

The door opened. A large man in a badly tailored suit looked them over. "Who's this?"

"A companion." Martin forced his voice to be firm, clear, and dismissive.

"We were only told about one."

"Oh, just let them in," came a voice from inside the room.

The large man, it was a different large man every time, stood aside and Martin stepped in, taking comfort in Arthur being right behind him.

The room was cheap and tatty. Anything quality, right down to the gilt, had been stripped away years ago. He doubted anyone actually slept in the rooms. It had become a place for transactions such as these. Martin wanted to get out as fast as possible.

"Mr. Jones," Martin said with a nod. He was more than familiar with 'Mr. Jones' real name and record but pretended that he wasn't. At least for as long as Mr. Jones was useful.

The door snicked shut behind them. Martin balled his hands into fists in his pockets. There was no way he could handle this. He should have sent Mr. Abram to pick up the piece and risk losing the money if it was wrong.

"Already unwrapped for your inspection."

Martin glanced at the art standing up on a cheap armchair. He had last seen it in a minimalist white frame. There was no frame now and an obvious yellow of nicotine stained the whites and pastels. He grabbed on to the small spark of anger, hoping he could flame it enough to override the fear that was crawling up his throat and trying to choke the very breath from him.

"Not your usual type, I've got to say."

Martin nodded a bit, but the Agnes Martin had hung in pride of place over the never-used fireplace, distinctly different from the collection of impressionist and inter-war surrealists. He had stared at it as he cried at sixteen, once again ripped from his home and transplanted to another. It had not been a healthy home, but it was an environment he was used to.

He took a small folding magnifying glass from his pocket. He didn't need it. He could tell from the other side of the room it was what he was looking for, but he had to make a show of it. A buyer for a wealthy reclusive art collector. He brought down every ounce of Agency training to keep his hands still. He wanted to scream. He could feel his skin crawl. "It will require cleaning."

"Hey, you just said an Agnes Martin named "Untitled" and gave a vague description. Do you know how many paintings that lady didn't bother to title?"

Martin gave what he hoped was a dry look. "Wrap it for me." He took a roll of cash from the pocket of his coat and tossed it to Mr. Jones.

Martin checked on Arthur. He and the large man were eyeballing each other but things didn't feel like they were heading south, yet.

"In a hurry?"

"Reservations."

The painting was quickly wrapped in brown paper and twine. "A pleasure, as always, Mister Green."

Martin nodded and picked up the painting, trying not to give the impression that he was running or that a panic attack was swirling below the surface. Arthur followed him out, down the steps and to the waiting car. The painting just managed to fit in the trunk.

As the car pulled away from the curb, something broke loose in him and his breath began to speed out of control while his body vibrated at a painful rate.

"Martin?"

He turned to Arthur.

"What do you need from me right now?"

Martin shook his head. The panic had stolen the words from him. Arthur held out his hands, palm up. Martin gripped them tight.

"Okay, do you think you can follow my breathing?"

Martin shook his head again.

"Okay, can you feel my hands?"

Martin nodded and squeezed them a little tighter.

"Good, focus on my hands. They're warm and they're not going anywhere. I'm going to talk, try to latch on to what I'm saying."

Martin nodded.

"We are in a very nice car driving through New York. There is the faintest fall of snow. It makes the city look clean, like something out of a movie. No one has taken down their Christmas decorations yet, so everything still has colored lights and tinsel. It's beautiful. It's cold outside, but not the prairie cold I grew up with. That will freeze your eyeballs. It's just cold enough to make you want hot chocolate, a heavy blanket, and a good book."

Martin could feel his breathing begin to slow as he lost himself in Arthur's words.

"I can see why people live here. I could almost live here myself, but maybe only in winters. I hear the summers are sticky and awful."

Martin had a flash, remembering his first summer in the city, so different from what he had known.

"I know I don't normally comment on what you wear, but I noticed your suit today. Hard not to. Gives you this aura of authority. Somehow your posture looks even better, and you've got the posture of a dancer."

Martin had never really considered his posture before. He was sure he'd been told to sit up straight a few times in his life but more often he'd been told to sit still.

"I'm sure the city is going to be a drunken zoo tomorrow, New Year's Eve and all, but if you'd be up for one excursion, the IFC is going to be screening *Casablanca*. I don't know if you've seen it, but it's a classic."

Martin gave his head a little shake. "Haven't seen it." There was a raspy croak in his voice like he'd been crying. He put one hand to his face to feel for tears, but it came back dry.

"Hey, it's okay. Are you settled enough for a proper hug?"

Martin nodded. He hated that Arthur had to ask, hated that he knew to ask. That he'd seen Martin reflexively try to throw his still damaged body across the room, his mind filled with the sensations of things not there.

Arthur scooted over and pulled him close. He put his face to the crook of Arthur's neck, focusing on the pulse he felt beneath the skin and his unique smell of faint spices and oils that never seemed to fade no matter how long he was away from a kitchen or however much soap and aftershave he used.

He stayed there, breathing slowly until the car pulled to a stop and the engine was turned off.

Chapter Sixteen

STILL HOLDING MARTIN TIGHT, Arthur glanced out the window of the town car. If he had to guess, he'd say they were at a storage facility, a very fancy storage facility. Though he wasn't sure what he expected, considering he just watched Martin throw a very thick-looking roll of cash to a seedy looking guy in an incredibly sleazy hotel room.

Martin pulled away, wiped his face, and with a couple of well-placed tugs, straightened his suit back to its prior sharpness. He took a deep breath and got out of the car. Arthur slid out behind him, not wanting him out of reach. A man approached them. Instead of the heavy work clothes he would expect from the industrial-looking area they were surrounded by, the man was in a heavy suit and wearing white gloves.

"Mister Grove," the man greeted them.

Martin only gave the man a small nod. The trunk was opened and the man carefully took out the painting.

No words were spoken as the man led them through the facility. Instead of hallways of rattling metal doors that one would ordinarily find in a storage facility, each door looked heavy and fireproof. From his work at the Agency, Arthur recognized some of the security they passed through and took note that the instructions for fire were to evacuate individual rooms because the air would be sucked out.

They stopped in front of a door.

"We can take it from here."

"Of course, Mr. Grove." The man gently handed Arthur the painting, probably assuming Arthur was some sort of assistant, and left.

Martin swiped a card to one lock, pressed his thumb to another, then keyed in sixteen digits on a pad. The door clicked open. Martin opened it and Arthur was hit by cool dry air. For the few seconds before lights flickered on, he felt like he was walking into a tomb.

"You can put it on the table," Martin said as he closed the door. There was another hiss and Arthur's ears actually popped. Arthur looked around. The room was full of paintings, but not hanging on the walls. Instead, they were sideways on racks like coats waiting to be tried on. He could see how each hanger could be rolled out to view a painting, front and back.

Martin sat hard in a chair and stripped off the brown paper from the painting. "Shit." Arthur looked up, trying to decide if that was the first time he'd ever heard Martin swear. "Really, who buys an Agnes Martin then smokes under it? The whole point of this painting is the fine subtleties of the pastels against the white canvas. This is going to need so much cleaning."

Arthur had no answer since he didn't know who the artist in question was, though he could see that there was a light yellow-brown across it. A color he mostly recognized from his father's fingers.

Martin took out that magnifying glass again and was looking closely at the edges, possibly trying to work out the depth of damage. Arthur carefully pulled out a large painting that was hanging at the far end of the racks. A young girl in an old fashion ballet costume was caught mid-pirouette. The brush strokes were heavy, giving movement to the figure, but not detail.

"Martin, is this a Degas?" Arthur heard his voice crack.

"Is it a ballet dancer?" Martin didn't look up from his work.

"Yes?"

"Then it's a Degas."

A strange headache that had been threatening pretty much since he'd seen the *Le Viandier de Taillevent* finally bloomed between his eyes. He sat down at the table across from Martin. Martin didn't even look up, still focused on the nicotine-stained pastels.

"Martin, not to be crass, but... yeah, this is going to be crass, and I'm sorry but I need to ask, how rich are you?"

Martin straightened up before making a sound that was somewhere between a laugh and a sigh. He rubbed at his face for a minute. To Arthur, it seemed like he was trying to scrub something from it. "Extremely," Martin finally answered.

"Okay." He didn't want to push, he really didn't, he never pushed Martin, but he'd handled a 15th-century cookbook before lunch, had just touched a Degas ballet dancer, and was pretty sure the strangely shaped bull glaring at him from the painting at the end of the rack was a Picasso.

Martin sighed and rolled his shoulders, then shook his hands hard for a split second in a way Arthur had never seen. Almost like he was trying to snap them into place.

"From what I was able to gather, my mother and my aunt did not have happy childhoods. My mother ran away and found the Reverend and the Farm. My aunt came here and found a much older man who was, in a way, very like a medieval king, refusing to believe that his lack of an heir was his fault, so instead he married and divorced a progression of increasingly younger women. He came from money so old and covered in blood you'd never be able to find where it started. My aunt managed to stay married long enough to outlive him without producing children, but the damage was done. By the time my mother died and the farm was raided, my aunt was busy converting liquid assets into prescription pharmaceuticals and high-end alcohol. I think child services saw the penthouse, diamond bracelet, and staff when they dropped me off and didn't check anything else. One more child off the books. She didn't even know who I was the next morning. She didn't get as far as liquidating the real estate or selling the jewels before she overdosed."

Martin bit his lip for a second, another tick Arthur had never seen.

"I was sixteen when that happened. I instantly became wealthy enough that I could have legally emancipated myself, but my lawyer saw that it was obvious I didn't have the skills to survive on my own, even with my wealth. A society friend of my aunt's, her name was Alice, offered to take me in, give me a place so I could continue at the same school. She was very kind."

Martin's voice became soft for a moment and Arthur knew how that story ended.

"I had just turned eighteen, but hadn't finished school yet, when she took a vacation with her lover to New Orleans. Her husband followed her. I had only met him a couple of times. They'd been fighting over the divorce details for over two years. He killed them. Threw me out. A few years later, I was contacted by her estate and informed she was a third cousin of my aunt, and there was no other family. Once her husband had been found very guilty, her estate went to me. Except her husband had sold off basically everything by then. What cash he hadn't spent was permanently locked overseas. I don't care about the money, though."

Martin gestured to the room.

"Her art collection was her great passion. She gave me, I don't know if it counted as normal, but she gave me a couple of years of safety and stability when I needed it. She would have hated seeing her collection mistreated and scattered to the winds, so I've been trying to rebuild it piece by piece. Least I can do."

"Can I give you a hug?" Arthur asked. He always asked.

"Yes."

Arthur crouched down next to Martin so he could pull him in close while trying to process a life so violently yanked from one place to another. "I'm sorry," he whispered.

"For what?"

"Everything you've had to go through."

Martin just shrugged. "There are those who live through far worse every day. My life has left me the final beneficiary of obscene quantities of wealth built on generations of abuse and human misery, and I've never known what to do with it and have tried to live without it."

"The financial aspect is being taken care of?" Arthur repeated what had been told to the library children.

"My lawyer was surprised, to say the least. I've only ever touched the assets to maintain the library endowment here. Now I'm telling him that I plan to send potentially dozens of children to the most elite private schools. We may have to eventually sell one of the park side buildings to do it."

"*One* of the park side buildings?"

Martin shrugged again looking a bit embarrassed, and it was Arthur's turn to laugh a little. "Okay. And the art? I don't think this will all fit in your apartment when you're done."

"There were a couple of small museums that Alice particularly liked. The kind that would never be able to afford a Degas that came up for auction. When the collection is finished, I will loan it in her name."

"Even your cancan dancer?"

Martin ran his thumb along the edge of the painting. This close, Arthur could smell the residue of nicotine covering the barely-there pinks and yellows.

"No. That one I'll keep. She might actually be a distant relative. And I've gotten used to her."

"So have I." Arthur gave Martin another squeeze then sat back down. "I'm sorry I pushed. I shouldn't have."

Martin shook his head. "It's okay. I've wanted to tell you. Lots of things I've wanted to tell you. It's just hard."

"I understand. I... I've been thinking, I'm not great at putting words to feelings either but you should know, I'm not planning on going anywhere, not unless you send me away. You smooth out the jagged bits in my brain. I don't know how, but you do." Martin reached across the painting and took his hand.

"I fully realized today that the thought that you might not be with me in the library next winter was an intolerable one."

A knot formed in Arthur's throat that he tried to swallow around. "How bad would it be if I cried on this painting?" he managed to choke out.

"Nothing that couldn't be fixed."

"I'll still try to avoid it."

Martin lowered his head, his grip still tight. "I do not know how much longer I can stay with the Agency." The words were soft but clear. Arthur found no shock in them.

"Because of what happened?"

"In part. It will be some time, if ever, before I'm able to perform my job at peak ability again. However, there are some things I need to do there first. I have never needed the Agency. Technically I have never needed any employment. The Agency found me. Alone, intelligent, low social skills, according to my recruitment profile. They offered me structure, while staying within the bubble of my own mind."

"Then I showed up and popped that bubble."

Martin looked up at him. He had a small smile and a shine in his eyes. "No. You sat quietly beside me until our bubbles merged into one."

Arthur could not suppress his grin. "That's one of the most romantic things anyone's ever said to me."

Martin squeezed his hands. "There are other things, but I no longer feel tied to the Agency as I once did."

"You've got my support. I'm an indentured servant there for a few more years since they covered my grad school, but I will support whatever you want to do. What will you do? I don't think you'd be good at being idle rich."

"I'm not sure."

"Teach?" That was the obvious one.

"Perhaps. But there are few places where I could teach the way I am accustomed to, add to that..."

"Library kids."

"Yes."

Arthur looked around. "Fine art dealing?"

Martin half chuckled "Only if you come to shady backroom trade-offs with me."

"Something with books?"

"Maybe. I do enjoy books."

A strange little thought fluttered across Arthur's mind. Martin's kitchen as he'd first encountered it. "When you were being forced to leave, by any chance did you take a silver knife, fork, spoon, and some china along with the cancan dancer?"

A smile touched Martin's lips and there was a glint in his eye. "It's hard to get full price for antique silver sets when three pieces are missing."

The original plans were for a particularly well-known French bistro for lunch and an Ethiopian place he'd read about online for dinner, but Arthur could see the stress settling across Martin's shoulders. He couldn't deny feeling rattled himself, what with the shady backroom art dealing and the emotional confessions done over a painting that was easily worth more than he made in a year or three.

There was also an energy building in the city. Even though it was another day before New Year's Eve, the streets seemed more crowded and parties looked to be spilling out of places, for good or ill. Occasionally there would be the crack and bang of a premature firework echoing around the buildings.

When they got back to the hotel, Martin didn't object in the slightest to the idea of ordering room service and watching documentaries about the history of glass and the evolution of domestic dogs.

They were stretched out in the large bed when Martin dozed off in the middle of a soft voiced explanation about how the shift from hunter-gatherers to agricultural societies forwarded the necessity for written language.

Arthur picked up his phone and flicked open his messages to Carol.

I think I just told Martin I want to spend the rest of my life with him.

It took about thirty seconds before he got back a string of wedding themed emojis.

No. We were just making sure we were on the same emotional page with each other.

Boo. I want to be your maid of honor. I own a rainbow tux.

That image settled into Arthur's head and refused to dislodge itself.

I won't ask why.

It was pride. There were a few more relevant emojis. **How's NY?**

Haven't seen much yet. Managed to ride the subway and eat good pizza. The MET is cool. Have you ever been here?

There was a delay, then a photo came through. Arthur squinted at it, then zoomed in. It was a diploma from NYU, with Carol's name on it.

You knew I was going to New York! You could have spent the last month telling me all your favorite places!

I spent four years living off instant noodles from the bodega. I would get a hot dog with peppers when I felt the malnutrition start to set in.

Arthur shook his head.

I'll see if I can smuggle you a pizza across state lines.

And when you and Martin decide you need to file paperwork, Jen and I will be witnesses.

Arthur looked down at Martin, sleeping half-curled against his side.

Thanks.

Chapter Seventeen

MARTIN AWOKE TO THIN light coming between the curtains and a note from Arthur saying he was popping downstairs to the deli on the corner and would bring back breakfast. He was fairly certain it was the sound of the bedroom door softly closing that had woken him.

He sat up then leaned slowly forward, trying to touch his toes. In the past, he had not put much thought into his physical strength or flexibility beyond what was required to pass annual checks to maintain his various levels within the Agency.

His physical therapist had encouraged him to try to gain muscle in his legs as it would help support the twisted joints that would likely take several years to fully heal. He hoped his legs were strong enough for his upcoming plans.

He heard a crack in the distance. The sun was barely up and people were already setting off fireworks.

He took more long breaths and tried to continue through basic stretches. It had been a while since he'd had a day as mentally draining as the one before. Somehow, they always left his body aching, as if he'd been running like a mad thing for too long.

He heard the elevator door open and the sound of soft and steady footfalls. Arthur popped his head into the bedroom. "Hey, you're awake."

"Yes."

"I've got breakfast when you feel like getting up. Or, if you like, you can have breakfast in bed."

Martin shook his head. He mostly associated eating in bed with being sick or injured.

Arthur had gone a little overboard at the deli, bringing back four different types of bagels as well as a couple of breakfast sandwiches he eagerly tucked into.

Martin picked out a plain bagel and a small container of salmon spread.

"How are you feeling today?" Arthur asked as he sipped coffee from a paper cup, despite the high end, in-room coffee maker five feet away.

Martin did a quick appraisal of himself, head to toe, then took a mental step back and scanned over his emotional state as well. That had been a hard but necessary skill to learn. "I'm... well. I'm better."

"Good."

"I think I should contact the woman who sent that letter."

Arthur froze, his coffee halfway to his lips. "Okay." He dragged out the word. "And what is the plan for that?"

"I think it would be best if I made the call from my lawyer's office, in case his counsel is needed. I would like you there as well."

"Of course. Absolutely."

"Thank you." Martin wasn't sure when he'd fully decided to make the call. Probably sometime the day before in between panic attacks and emotional truths, but he didn't want it hanging over his head, an unanswered question mark in his life.

"It's already getting a bit crowded out there. Do you think you'll be up for going out today?" Arthur asked.

"Yes." He knew Arthur wanted to introduce him to a classic film. He'd actually heard of *Casablanca*, and even had a vague idea of the plot. Something about French resistance fighters trying to escape North Africa during World War II and using a bar as their base. Maybe?

They dressed warmly as they headed out. The streets were getting crowded, even miles from Times Square and moving in the opposite direction. He never understood why people came to New York in the middle of winter to stand around in the cold and watch a lit-up ball get slowly lowered. But there were a lot of things he still didn't understand.

Even as a grown and arguably successful adult, he still found himself trying to work out things from context clues. He hadn't been aware of how much he didn't know or understand on the farm, but that was the point of the place.

The family he was temporarily placed with for two months had been nice enough, but they didn't understand why he didn't talk beyond the prayers over meals. He remembered hearing the word trauma a lot. They didn't understand that he didn't understand any of it, from electricity, to eggs in a carton, to milk in cardboard. He had no frame of reference for even starting to ask the questions.

In retrospect, he was lucky the raid came at the beginning of summer. He would have never managed school when he was still scared of lamps that lit themselves at the touch of a button. Not to mention cars. At least that family had a garden. Over two months, he methodically removed every slug, snail, and pest by hand and was only annoyed there were no chickens to feed the slugs to.

And if those days had been a nightmare of confusion, the city was hell. There were moments in the first few days when he thought that maybe he had died without the Time of Confession and the social worker had transported his soul to hell. He still cringed internally at the sound of his classmates' laughter when he didn't know who the president was. Luckily, the question had been phrased in such a way that he didn't have to reveal that he didn't know *what* a president was.

He'd spent those first few school years yanking books from the library shelves a dozen at a time, desperately trying to fill in the gaps, but it never fully helped. There was always something *new*. Television he didn't watch, movies he wasn't taken to and didn't know to take himself, music he didn't listen to, fresh layers of culture and media created and blended at a rate he could never keep up with. When the Agency's recruiter made it very clear that they did not care that he had never seen *Titanic,* it had been a relief beyond measure. He stopped trying to fill in those gaps and allowed himself to settle into the comfortable acquisition of well-researched knowledge for his own pleasure and at his own pace.

Until a man who loved old movies, pulp novels, and food from everywhere sat across from him at lunch. He never told Arthur that *Gilda* was only the 23rd film he'd ever seen (not that he could remember most of it, his head and heart had felt so broken that night). The rest were from Movie Days at school or the occasional movie night in university where an enthusiastic RA drove him down to sit with dorm mates.

Arthur pressed close to him to make space for a group of already intoxicated women coming towards them. They were covered in glitter and passing a bottle of champagne between them.

"Happy New Year!" one of them screamed in Arthur's general direction.

"Happy New Year," Arthur replied with a smile before they turned to descend into the subway. They took the same route as Arthur's first night in the city. The train rattled and the cars were packed to capacity, but they would never get there in time trying to drive. He squeezed himself tightly against Arthur as they held the same pole and grabbed his hand as they were jostled by other passengers onto the platform at their stop.

A gust of crisp air across his face managed to pull in his focus.

"I think you'll like this," Arthur said as they stood in line for tickets. "There's a bit of a MacGuffin, but really it's a study of character in times of stress or crisis."

"What's a MacGuffin?"

"It's an apparatus for trapping lions in the Scottish Highlands," the man standing in line behind them said.

Martin turned. "But—"

Arthur put a hand on his shoulder and waved the other man away. "I'll explain later, it's just a film term, not important." Arthur ordered two tickets and one popcorn. Martin had never warmed up to popcorn. The crunch and salt and butter would be fine, and then one piece would squeak on his teeth in just the wrong way and it would make him feel as if his whole skeleton was getting an electric shock.

The lights dimmed and the projector sprang to life. He knew Arthur owned this movie. He had seen it on a shelf in his apartment tucked in with dozens of others, but there were some that Arthur insisted were better 'in a proper theater.'

Around him he could hear people whispering along to the dialogue, having obviously memorized every word. He tried to focus on the plot and how Arthur was holding his hand.

He'd been wrong about the plot. So wrong. It wasn't about resistance fighters; it was about broken hearts and people convincing themselves that alone was better than risking showing who they truly were to anyone else.

He turned his head briefly towards the end to catch Arthur wiping his eyes as a plane took off into an improbably foggy night.

When Rick and Louis walked away side-by-side and the final title card came up with the swell of *La Marseillaise*, he wondered what the first audience was supposed to believe happened next. The US had not even entered the war when the film was being made. There was the drumbeat of patriotism, but no guaranteed victory. The disillusioned

American taking up the fight and the Frenchman throwing off his loyalty to the Vichy government was an obvious metaphor, but what of Rick and Louis? Of the beautiful friendship? Was the audience meant to think that their friendship would last through the war? Would it go beyond? Would they reign over some post-war Paris or New York nightclub together? Rick and Louis Place with Sam still at the piano?

The lights rose and people stood around them. Martin turned to Arthur. "Were Rick and Louis in love?"

Arthur smiled brightly. "I think Louis was very in love with Rick, in his own way, and they telegraphed it as much as the censors at the time would allow. I also think Rick was too damaged to notice if someone gave a shit about him, and Louis knew that, but that didn't mean he didn't try."

"Round up the usual suspects?"

"I think that might be when Rick started getting a clue." Arthur stood and Martin followed. "There's a diner that looks really good a couple of blocks over. Want to grab something to eat before heading back to the hotel?"

"Sure." He did not actually feel particularly hungry, but he had no desire to deny Arthur these simple pleasures, especially when they would be eating dinner in to avoid the New Year's crowd.

There was a table for two available. Arthur ordered a thick tuna melt and a slice of pie. Martin ordered the chicken salad sandwich. He knew the smile Arthur sent his way was one of pride. Being proud of him.

Martin could remember staring at a similar menu before their first movie. The words had swirled and his eyes hadn't been able to focus on anything. The only decision he had made that day was to skip work and buy alcohol, which he hadn't drunk. Being asked to choose food? He had worried for a second that he was perhaps having a stroke or neurological incident. Arthur had taken the menu from his hands and ordered for both of them, but it hadn't felt like an act of dismissal or frustration, rather one of kindness, doing the thinking for both of them on a day when he simply couldn't.

Perhaps that night was the start of their Beautiful Friendship. Arthur had already shown him kindnesses the way few others had, but something had changed that night when Arthur came looking for him, found him so deep in grief and pain he could barely form words. He had somehow known what Martin needed even if Martin couldn't work it out himself. He had given him the right combination of kindness and strength, protection and freedom.

It was later, almost too long later, when he realized what the combination of feelings that swirled in him must mean. He knew he would have to talk to Arthur about who he was and what he felt and what he could and could not give. Then that damned assignment had come around and he hadn't had time to find the right words. Just a few sentences in the Agency hallway that he wasn't even sure Arthur understood.

All his time away, trapped in a nightmare, he had hoped Arthur understood.

"Do you have a copy of *Gilda*?" Martin asked as their food arrived.

Arthur looked at the ceiling, thinking. "I *think* so. I think it's part of a Rita Hayworth box set I have. If it's not, I can easily get it."

"I would like to see it again. I can't seem to remember pieces of it, so the plot doesn't fully make sense when I think about it."

Arthur's smile was a gentle one. "You had other things on your mind. When we get home, we can curl up on the couch and watch it one evening."

"That sounds nice."

The chicken sandwich was good, and he had half of Arthur's pie.

Chapter Eighteen

THE FROZEN WIND NIPPED at Arthur's nose, but he didn't particularly care. They hadn't stayed up until midnight to ring in the New Year by choice. The fireworks had simply made it impossible to sleep. Still, when midnight ticked over, Martin had leaned in and put a tiny kiss high on his cheek, almost at his ear, then wished him Happy New Year. It had left Arthur lying awake for an hour, blinking into the darkness of the room.

For them, day-to-day physical intimacy was holding hands. If emotions were running high, there might be a hug or it might mean they sat with a table between them and breathed together.

Arthur knew early on that Martin was offering his mind and heart, but his body was off limits and he had accepted that without a second thought. Martin's heart and mind were an amazing and precious gift that he treasured every moment. But even as the wind numbed his face, he could still feel where that little peck had been. There was so much in the way of an 'average' life Martin had never experienced, maybe he had wanted to try something as close to a New Year's kiss as he felt comfortable with. Maybe he was worried that Arthur was expecting one. Arthur hoped not. He would hate if Martin tried to push himself beyond where he felt comfortable. He knew it was a big conversation they should have already had but, for now, he just listened to the rhythm of their steps on the icy gravel of Central Park.

There were a surprising number of museums and shops open on New Year's Day. They had spent the morning browsing in and out of them, getting breakfast and lunch from steaming carts on the sidewalk. Then Martin had turned them to a kitchen supply store and Arthur had nearly died as he wondered how many restaurant-quality pans he could fit in his luggage and how much of his 401k he could spend on knives. And how many knives could he put in his luggage before the TSA got annoyed? Did he need a whole new set of kitchen knives? No. Did he want them? Yes.

"Are we looking for something in particular?" Arthur asked Martin, trying to hold in his excitement. It would be nice if Martin was looking for things for himself.

"I need to get a knife for someone, then go to see them. Do you mind helping?"

"No?" Who did Martin know in New York who needed a knife?

He took a basic chef knife from a display row and handed it to Arthur. "One like this, but something that will last."

Well, this was Arthur's wheelhouse. He held the blade in his hand, then put it back. Fortunately, he'd done this before Christmas when assembling Martin's gift. He scanned his eyes along the brand names. Expensive wasn't always best.

"That one." He pointed to a chef knife in the display case. "Not too heavy but holds an edge well."

Martin motioned the clerk over to pay for the knife, even wrap it, then went outside and flagged down a cab. Arthur's curiosity was absolutely clawing at him, but Martin seemed calm. Or rather, he didn't seem to be putting on any front or character the way he had at the library or the art buy.

Eventually the cab dropped them off in an area of the city far from the tourist or business centers. It felt like an area where people simply worked and lived. Martin went up a couple of steps to an unassuming door and pressed a button.

"I'm not sure if she's in. I should have called ahead."

"Okay." Arthur still wasn't sure who *she* was but was willing to wait.

There was the sound of footfalls on the other side of the door. The snick of a peep hole cover and then the clicks of various locks. The door opened, revealing a small woman with gray hair. She looked Martin up and down. "You are still in New York?"

"Yes."

She looked Arthur over next. "Who is this?"

"This is Arthur. He's been teaching me to cook. Arthur, this is Tala."

Arthur felt Tala's hard eyes scrutinizing every inch of him. He didn't flinch. It was the same look Hanh had given him every time he stepped into her line of sight. He knew any show of weakness would be unacceptable but he also had to acknowledge that he was in no way in charge of the situation.

She gestured them inside with a nod of her head. With only a few steps, they were in a small kitchen. Martin handed her the gift box. She opened it carefully.

"The handle on your knife was broken."

She nodded and placed the knife on the table. She looked over Arthur again. "What do you cook?"

The tone was somewhere between job interview and a 'what are your intentions' grilling.

"I have professional training in Vietnamese cuisine with a grounding in classical French. I'm competent in most pastries but have never been great at tempering chocolate."

Tala waved a dismissive hand in his direction, then she pointed at Martin. "He needs proper food. See if you can learn adobo."

Before Arthur could comment that he had made adobo before, a few different varieties, she reached into her fridge and pulled out a chicken with the head and feet still attached. She put it on the table in front of him along with a cutting board and a knife with a broken handle.

"Pieces, now."

"Yes, ma'am." He glanced over at Martin as he quickly broke down the chicken. Martin smiled at him over a cup of thick black coffee and decided that whatever he was about to learn or go through would be worth it.

Martin hadn't anticipated that Tala would demand to give Arthur a cooking lesson right there, but he also wasn't surprised. She was protective that way. She hadn't been able to fold him in with her own sons, older than him, boisterous, popular in their circles, but she had tried.

Arthur had completed every task she set him with the dedication of a dinner rush. He had stood there and sipped coffee and mostly watched Arthur's hands. There was efficiency in every movement, but also grace. He wondered how many cuts and burns it had taken to develop that.

During the hours when the chicken was marinating, she lectured Arthur on other dishes Martin had never known the names of, but that she remembered feeding him.

When the chicken was finally ladled over rice, she declared it 'not bad for a first try.' Martin had to hold back a rush of sense memory at the first bite, sequestered in the kitchen, away from some fancy party, his school uniform shoes feeling heavy on his feet. The sound of Tala's voice as she ordered around the servers hired for the party, yet every time she walked by him, she would lay a comforting hand on his back and make a little shushing noise like she was trying to calm a skittish animal or a crying child. Maybe he *had* been crying. He couldn't remember that clearly.

It was dark when Tala finally ushered them out the door. He had texted for the town car to be waiting, knowing it would be hard to flag down a cab in the area and it could be a long wait between trains.

"Okay," Arthur said with a sigh as he leaned back in the seat. "Who exactly was that?"

"Tala."

"And how does she fit in your life?"

"She was my aunt's housekeeper. She..."

"She took care of you."

"Yes."

"So, my cooking skills just got thoroughly evaluated by the closest thing to a mother you have."

"Yes."

"Did I pass?"

"It would make me very happy if you could make adobo again some time."

Arthur took his hand. "Any time you like."

For the next few days Martin let himself be guided almost blindly from one end of New York to the other in a way he didn't think would be possible. They bounced from the MoMA to the Museum of Mathematics. They ate in tiny restaurants that sat four and some of the most famous New York culinary establishments. (He wished Arthur had given him that list of his. He could have made reservations in the more prestigious locations).

Arthur bought postcards and fridge magnets and a t-shirt with a pizza on it from a sidewalk table. He'd held it up and asked if he thought it would fit Carol. Martin had no idea.

And in the moments when he felt his own energy begin to flag, or the crowds or bustle became too much, Arthur always seemed to know and, without a word between them, he would suddenly find himself in a quiet corner of a museum or holding a cup of tea at a tiny table in the back of a diner with Arthur just waiting, no urgency in his manner or form.

Sometimes in those moments there would be seconds where he could not breathe for the waves of feelings that crashed over him. He'd gone through his life taking advice from few, orders from many. Often feeling little more than numb from day to day. Then Arthur had held out his hand and sat down for lunch. And here Arthur still was. Quietly sitting with him while snow dusted the streets and sidewalks of New York City.

He took his hand from his teacup and placed it around Arthur's. Arthur smiled and another wave crashed. He was sure love was too small a word for what he was feeling. A binding from which he never wanted to be unbound. A sea into which he desired to sink. He laced his fingers into Arthur's and squeezed hard. He knew he must be causing pain but right now he didn't have the words, didn't know if there were words, and could only hope that Arthur would understand.

Arthur squeezed his hand in return. Firm but more gently than his own desperate grasp. "It's okay," he said softly, then slowly took Martin's other hand and guided it to the side of his neck.

He could feel Arthur's pulse, fast, but strong and steady, and knew he was understood.

Chapter Nineteen

It was still early, even for the city that never sleeps, when they arrived at Mr. Abram's office. He wanted to get this done early. He had plans for later in the day and if he spun out (it had been all he could do to fight back an anxiety attack the night before), he wanted to have time to recover.

Mr. Abram looked Arthur over. "So, this is the husband. When do I get to meet the thirty kids?" Arthur looked flustered and Martin huffed. "You know I'm teasing you." He held out his hand. "Philip Abram."

"Arthur Dram."

Mr. Abram gestured them to the desk. "It's nice to meet you. I've heard a lot about you and by a lot I mean two whole sentences, but that is more than anyone else has ever gotten, ever."

Arthur shrugged a bit and looked a little shy as they took their seats.

Martin could feel his nerves beginning to rise and took long slow breaths through his nose so as not to alert the other two.

Mr. Abram looked at him. "I would like to state officially as your lawyer and unofficially as someone who has known you for a very long time that you don't have to do this. I can send a letter. You keep me on retainer to deal with things like this."

"Not things like this," Martin replied softly. There was nothing like this. You can't send lawyers to fight childhood ghosts.

Arthur took his hand. "I'm right here and I'll hang up if you start to spin out." Martin took a deep breath and nodded. Mr. Abram shook his head and dialed the number at the bottom of the letter.

The phone rang. Martin didn't believe in prayer or luck, but every so often he still found himself wishing and he wished for voice mail.

"Hello?" came a woman's sleepy voice from the speakers.

"Is this Grace Howard?"

"Yes?"

"This is Philip Abram. I am the legal counsel for Mr. Grove. He is here with his partner, and he is willing to speak to you."

"Oh... Um.... Okay. Hello Martin."

"Hello." Martin scoured his mind for the name Grace Howard, but so many of the girls had names like Grace, Hope, Faith, and Angel. And so many of his memories were lost to a haze of willful forgetfulness.

"Um... Not sure you remember me by name, but I was about a year older than you. Red hair. My mother and I were the only two red heads on the farm."

A slight memory began to form. A girl with red braids, her hands caked in mud. "Yes. I remember you. They would make you chop wood and dig the garden with the grown men."

"Trying to burn the energy out of me. You were one of the quiet ones. You could get the eggs from the chickens without getting the shit scratched out of you."

A memory of warm, fresh laid eggs, delicate in his hands. "You just had to scratch them under the chin and make little clucking noises."

"It was still only you."

There was silence on the line for long moments and Martin thought perhaps they had been disconnected. "May I ask why you are contacting me?"

Grace sighed. "Sorry. The church part of the farm went on for another five or so years after the cops raided. Only stopped after a second raid. You and a few others were long gone by then but, sorry, you said there were other people there. Years of therapy and I still have problems talking to Empties. Sacred Silence and all that bullshit."

Martin turned to Arthur who looked confused but was still holding his hand. "Arthur is my partner. We met at work. He likes old movies, cooking, and played Dungeons and Dragons in high school to rebel against a religiously conservative household. Philip was my aunt's lawyer and has known me since not long after the raids. He has officially been my lawyer since I was sixteen. He was in love with my aunt but never did anything about it. Enjoys blockbuster action movies, and still plays Dungeons and Dragons but tells the other partners he's going golfing. I don't know if he can play golf."

Mr. Abram rolled his eyes before dropping his face in one hand. A chuckle came down the line. "Yeah, the farm did a number on all of us. Okay. I can send the nitty-gritty details to your lawyer if you like but short version: a big conglomerate wants to put a water pumping station and bottling plant outside of town. The EPA and water rights people are saying no. The Business Association and some astroturf groups are saying yes. Ninety percent of the aquifer is under the farm and where the spring for the 'spring water' actually breaks the surface is about fifty yards behind the barn."

A map of the farm, distances twisted by childhood scale popped into his head. "The mud puddle in the apple orchard that the ducks always pooped in?"

"Crystal clear healthy spring water, according to the advertising markups. The court ordered that the landowners need to vote about what happens."

"Who are the landowners?"

There was another long pause. "The biological children of the Reverend."

Martin felt himself begin to shake slightly and Arthur squeezed his hand tight. "And who are they?"

"Put your hand flat on a table with your fingers loosely together."

"Okay." He placed the hand not being held by Arthur on the fine wood desk.

"Does your ring finger bend a little inwards and middle finger bend a little out, making for a gap, even though you've never broken them."

"Yes." Martin knew what was coming next. He had never asked his mother while she lived. Never looked fully at his own background check when he joined the Agency. He had never even seen his own birth certificate, the mess of acquiring one having been in Mr. Abram's hands all those years ago.

"It doesn't hold up in court. Need a DNA test, but so far we all—"

"I understand." For some reason the shaking had stopped and was being replaced by a cold numbness.

"Look, you can tell me to fuck off and plenty of others have. I've... I've learned to separate the Church and Reverend from the land. That apple orchard with the mud puddle is growing three types of rare breed apples. One of which is nearly extinct. The part of the farm that's still forest and fields has short ear owls, loggerhead shrike, queen snakes, all endangered or threatened, and all gone in a decade once they start pumping the water."

"I understand," Martin repeated. He could hear the flatness in his own voice in contrast to the hint of pleading in Grace's.

"If you like, I can communicate directly through your lawyer from now on." He felt Arthur take his other hand from the table and interlace the crooked fingers with his own. He felt so cold but knew that he wasn't.

"I... My therapist would encourage me to communicate directly whenever possible."

"Mine, too. I hate cold calling. Special level of hell."

"Yes. I will consider the situation and contact you when I have made a more detailed decision."

"Thank you." The line went dead.

Arthur did not hesitate to wrap his arms around him and pull him close. He closed his eyes and felt Mr. Abram drape a blanket around his shoulders even though the room was heated to a pleasant seventy-two. "You don't say goodbye because we will all meet again after the ascension," Martin muttered, half to himself.

"Old habits die hard."

"Yes."

"Proud of you," Arthur whispered in his ear. "Love you."

"Love you too," Martin whispered back and felt the numbness slowly begin to lift, even as tears fell.

Arthur was sure that after a phone call with his deep past, Martin wouldn't be up for doing anything but going back to their hotel and spending the day curled up in bed.

Instead, Martin's lawyer had let him take a nap on a very comfortable looking couch, giving the impression it wasn't the first time, while he and Arthur had talked about Dungeons and Dragons. Apparently, it was up to five editions. He couldn't talk about Martin's past any more than Arthur could talk about Martin's present, but they still managed to talk around some things. If Tala was meeting Mom, that was meeting Dad, or at least older brother.

When Martin finally woke up, looking a little the worse for wear, but not awful, he said he had something he'd like to do after lunch.

"You mentioned this," Martin said with an almost grand sweep of his arm. "And my leg is feeling okay today. I'd like you to teach me to skate."

Arthur looked across the glittering Rockefeller Center ice rink.

"I would love to." When Arthur had checked for tickets a few weeks earlier, he'd found the tickets completely sold out and had mentally set it aside for some unknown time in the future. Martin must have gotten them months in advance. It had actually been awhile since he'd laced on a pair of skates. University, if he recalled, but he was fairly certain some things lived in muscle memory. He looked at Martin still fiddling with his laces. "Here, let me. You really need to have your ankles supported."

Now Arthur was having college date flashbacks. A girl from his freshman economics class. She had argued passionately about Keynesian economics while everyone else just needed three credits for their degrees. He had taken her skating, which was fun, but he had felt nothing when she kissed him at the door of her dorm room.

Now Arthur *felt*. His heart felt large and warm as he helped Marten to his feet and held his hand as he took slow wobbling steps towards the ice. "Okay, you can grab the edge first while you find your center of balance." Arthur stepped onto the ice first, then Martin followed. For a second, he felt his legs wobble, then his core tightened and everything else relaxed.

He spun around and held out his hands. "It's okay. I won't let you fall."

Martin held out one gloved hand, then the other. "Don't lock your knees. Keep your core tight." Martin pushed off with one foot and wobbled, almost pulling Arthur over. "It's okay. Just do that again with the other foot. Push and glide. Let physics do the work for you."

Martin gave another little push and didn't wobble quite as much.

"See. Doing better already."

Martin smiled and squeezed his hands as he took tiny, hesitant glides while other skaters zipped by. A group of children with linked arms fell as one, laughing as they did.

"Want to try letting go of one hand? I'll skate beside you, and it'll give you a little more room."

Martin let go of one hand and instantly wobbled. Arthur caught it again. "Eyes up. Not at your feet. You don't have to look at your feet to walk and there's nothing to trip on, on the ice. Keep your eyes up and you'll keep your balance."

Martin nodded and slowly let one hand go again, managing to keep perfectly still. "Perfect." Martin's cheeks were red in the cold, but Arthur thought that under that red he could see a hint of blush.

Martin's movements were still slow and hesitant as they started their way around the rink side-by-side, but Arthur heaped on the praise. He couldn't help it and saw no reason why he should stop.

Less than a year ago he held Martin's hand in a hospital while Martin lay broken and emaciated. For months after, he jumped at shadows, and wept in the dark when he thought Arthur was asleep.

Now here he was, in the middle of New York City, trying something completely new, just because Arthur had mentioned it and it was something he had never experienced. With each slide across the ice, Arthur's heart felt like it would burst with pride.

Then, when they were finally gliding smoothly together, almost keeping pace with the slower skaters, Martin, slowly, and without a word, let go.

Arthur kept his hand out and didn't even attempt to remove what must have been the dumbest grin from his face. Ten feet down the ice, when Martin wobbled, his hand was there for a moment of balance and grounding before they took off again side by side.

And Arthur knew in his heart that they would come back and do this again. Each time a little stronger, a little better, and always side by side.

Epilogue

11 months later

"SINCE WE WILL BE deconstructing this into cubes as soon as it is cooled, is it entirely necessary to braid it?" Martin asked as he carefully coated his hands with flour per instructions. It was not an overly pleasurable feeling, but probably better than having the dough stick to his skin.

Carol measured out a sixth piece of dough onto Arthur's kitchen scale. "I have not done this since I was seventeen, which puts me on *very* thin ice with Nana Bloom. We are doing the braid today then turning it into stuffing tomorrow."

"You don't have to do this," Arthur tried to call out from his couch. "I will be fine tomorrow." Martin heard him take a breath mid-sentence. "And we'll have Thanksgiving in the cafeteria."

"You will not be fine tomorrow," Carol called back. "Because you have the flu."

"I do not. It's a little cold. And if I have the flu, why are you all here?"

"Because, when the memo went around, we all got our flu shots like good little government agents instead of waiting to catch it from a kid at the library."

Arthur muttered to himself. Two days earlier Martin had found him slumped over his keyboard with a fever of one hundred and three. He wondered if the flash of panic he had felt when brushing the burning skin was the same feeling Arthur had when he had found him passed out in his car.

That had caused a bio-contamination lockdown of the building of course, whereas Martin was quickly able to recognize the flu symptoms that had already taken down a number of agents. He'd flicked off a quick message to Arthur's supervisor and his own, then taken Arthur home to feed him chicken broth and acetaminophen.

He heard the door to Arthur's apartment open along with the rustlings of various bags. Doctor Jennifer Hernandez placed several grocery bags on the kitchen counter before collecting a quick kiss from her girlfriend.

"Okay," Jennifer pulled a bottle of Gatorade and a Blu-ray out of the last bag once the rest were emptied. "Explain to me how Mr. Movie over there has never seen *Jurassic Park*?"

"I grew up in a household where fossils were a creation of the Devil to lure the intelligent from the righteous path. Some things fell through the cracks." Arthur had uncurled himself from his place on the couch and stumbled into the kitchen.

Jennifer blinked at him a few times before shaking her head. "And I thought growing up Catholic was a trip."

He took the Gatorade from Jennifer and quickly chugged half the bottle. Martin could see where he had been sweating and knew the fever from earlier in the day must have finally broken, though if the pattern of the previous two days held, it would return in the evening.

Carol let out a long breath. "Well, it's going to become croutons." Martin looked over the challah bread and could give no judgment.

"Now what do we do?" he asked.

"Now we put it in a very low oven to rise, then wash our hands and go watch a movie that, while scientifically inaccurate, was very important at a pivotal stage in my life."

Martin was confused but was trying to be sociable and expand his own understanding of popular culture. He began washing the flour and dough from his hands.

"It gave you an interest in dinosaurs?" He did have a vague idea of the plot and it would explain her romantic involvement with a paleontologist.

"Less 'interest in dinosaurs' and more 'a sweaty Laura Dern running around in cargo shorts' let me answer a few important questions about myself."

Jennifer raised her hand and got a silent high five from Carol. Martin was still confused, and it must have shown on his face.

"They're lesbians and Laura Dern is hot," Arthur supplied between sips of Gatorade.

"Damn hot and particularly badass in this," Carol added as she slipped the bread into the slightly warm oven. "Okay, let's get Sicky back on the couch and non-feathery dinosaurs up on the screen."

"Not sick," Arthur mumbled even as he let Martin guide him to the nest of blankets.

Jennifer put the Blu-ray in and then joined Carol on the love seat, which didn't have the best view of the television, but Martin had no doubt they had both seen the film many times as they were humming along to the music playing under the menu options.

Arthur cuddled against his side before giving his hand a tight squeeze. "I'll be fine by next week."

"Of course you will," Martin said brushing his fingers through Arthur's hair, slicked down with sweat. They would be traveling to New York early that year to attend a hearing on Environmental Protection Agency vs. Black River Spring Water Incorporated. He felt it was important to attend since he had his own lawyers supporting the EPA case, but he had learned to be honest enough with himself to know that there was no way he could face a dozen half-siblings and the memories that came with them without Arthur holding his hand.

"I think your cancan girl would look really good there." Arthur gestured with his chin towards the empty wall over the love seats. His voice was rough and still tired from his third day of illness.

Martin laced their fingers together. He had thought that himself a time or two but had yet to bring up the courage to mention it. It would be simple to move. His possessions fit into one case plus a painting.

He had no intention of leaving Arthur and Arthur had said as much to him. Only the deep rut of habit kept them living apart.

Yes. That would be good. A step. A big one. A step that at one time would have been terrifying, but now he knew there were safe arms on the other side to catch him if he couldn't make it on his own. "We'll talk about it when you're feeling better." Arthur squeezed his hand and gave a sleepy smile. "For now, let's watch the movie."

About the Author

A psychologist once told Ada Maria Soto that she has a fantasy prone personality. Fortunately, Ada grew up to become an author, so a life lived deep in her imagination fits her perfectly. As a Mexican-American expat living in the South Pacific with her partner and kid, her life is chaotically divided between being a writer, a publisher, and a parent.

Dysgraphia, phonological dyslexia, and ADHD makes for some exciting editing, but Ada continues to push through with a writing career. She's a veteran of the theatre and television business, as well as all the lousy jobs that come with two liberal arts degrees.

Ada's ability to capture the complex inner life of her characters in moving, yet relatable, ways endears readers to her unforgettable characters. Whether writing hot, spicy erotica or "tame" romances about asexual characters, she creates stories that readers return to again and again.

When not buried under manuscripts, Ada is a sports fan dedicated to the Oakland A's, Auckland Blues, USA Eagles, and New Zealand Black Caps.

Also By Ada Maria Soto

Windsor Club
Tactical Submission
Triple Windsor

The Agency
His Quiet Agent
Merlin in the Library
Agents of Winter

Nested Hearts
Empty Nests
Bowerbirds

Eden Springs
Through the Dark Clouds
And Everything Nice
Life Saving Dal